DREW LECLAIR
GETS A CLUE

BY KATRYN BURY

CLARION BOOKS

An Imprint of HarperCollins*Publishers*

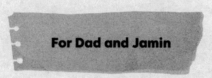

For Dad and Jamin

Clarion Books is an imprint of HarperCollins Publishers.

Drew Leclair Gets a Clue

ISBN: 978-0-35-874927-1

The text was set in Berling LT Std.
Cover design by Catherine San Juan
23 24 25 26 27   PC/CWR   10 9 8 7 6 5 4 3 2 1
First paperback edition, 2023

1

LITA MIYAMOTO SAYS THAT a good detective finds the puzzle pieces to solve a crime, but a *great* detective changes the puzzle. It's all about finding the right clues, she says—the clues that can actually *stop* something bad from happening again. Dr. Miyamoto is pretty much the greatest criminal profiler of all time and also my hero, so I'll take her word for it. I just wish I could go through my notebooks and figure out how to change the puzzle I call *Mom*.

Now that she is standing in the doorway, bags packed, and ready to leave, all I can think about are the clues I missed. Like when Mom freaked out about the empty bag of potato chips in the pantry. Or that she cried last week when I picked Dad's movie choice over hers. Or the night she didn't come home until after midnight and I saw her smiling in the hallway.

I'd missed every single one.

Which is super annoying, because I'm usually *great* at mysteries. Last year I tracked down a graffiti artist at school (an eighth-grade girl named Christina who made the mistake of using very obvious loops in her *y*'s and *s*'s), and I even solved the mystery of our neighbor Edna's missing rabbit this summer!

Maybe if I had profiled Mom, like Lita does with the criminals she tracks down, I could have stopped it. Or at least warned Dad.

"Drew. Look at me," she says, beckoning me to the door.

"Yeah, Mom?" I croak. A lump forms in my throat, but I refuse to let her see me upset.

Tears streak her pale and freckled cheeks. She's using her best sad face: searching eyes, one brow pulled down, and her lower lip trembling. I wonder if she would pass the lie detector test we took at the Spy Museum. Probably not. A mom who is actually sad about leaving wouldn't be *leaving*. And they certainly wouldn't be abandoning their family to live in a yurt in Kauai with their new boyfriend.

Yes, that's right. A *yurt*.

She told us about the whole plan on Friday and gave herself until today to "make arrangements." As if someone had died or something.

"Look. I've got to go, sweetheart." Her arms are still begging me for a hug, her long pianist fingers spread out urgently. "Remember, I love you. This isn't about you, or Dad. And it isn't about Mr. Clark."

Oh, yeah. Here's the best part: Mom isn't leaving with just anyone. Mr. Clark ("Dustin," as he insists I call him) is my guidance counselor. Or *was*, I guess, since he's joining Mom in their new hashtag-yurt life. He's been having conferences with Mom since the end of sixth grade to discuss my "social problems." Conferences, I realize now, that were probably not about me and mostly about *kissing*. Blech.

I force my mouth into a tight smile, as if I've accepted her nonapology. "Mm-hmm," I manage to grunt. "Have a safe flight."

Because I don't want her to get into a plane crash or anything. But I do hope there's lots of turbulence. And a really smelly guy sitting next to her.

Mom's eyes flash with disappointment. When Dad walks in from the hallway, she makes a big point of shrugging and gives him this look, as if asking him to solve the mystery of why I'm such a brat.

"Drew?" Dad says in a bone-weary voice. "Hug your mom goodbye, okay?"

My eyes flit to Dad, and then back to Mom. She's starting to look *really* sad now, but the thought of touching her gives me a stomachache.

"Bye. Tell Mr. Clark I said hi or whatever," I say, turning away. "I'll be in my room." Those last words are only for Dad, and she knows it.

Melodramatic sobs play me down the hallway like a guilt-trip opera, but I don't let it stop me. Stepping into my room, I slam the door and sit down at my desk as if nothing's different. Because, really, nothing is. This is all *so* Mom.

She's a repeat offender. And I know exactly how things will go. Dad will come into my room in approximately two minutes, tell me that Mom loves me, and give me a letter. Maybe this is the first time Mom has left for good, but it's not the first time she's taken little "vacations" from being a parent. Every time she does, she writes a letter. It's always handwritten and has all this lovey-dovey stuff that she never says to me in person. In fact, if Mom *were* a murderer, I'm pretty sure the Dear Drew letters would be her signature.

A criminal's signature, according to Lita Miyamoto,

is a pattern of things we do because we *need* to. As in, *really* need to. Like jewel thieves who leave a symbol at the scene of a crime or axe murderers who only use axes. Or like Mom. She doesn't actually murder people, but she does hurt everyone around her without ever saying sorry. So . . . close enough.

Lately I've been thinking that I don't even want her to live with us anymore.

The thought alone brings tears to my eyes. I *hate* crying. So I use my foolproof method to shut down the tears, perfected in fifth grade after dealing with two years of bullying. First I take three deep breaths. Then I try to focus on something else until the emotion dims.

My eyes snag on the picture of Mom and me at Disneyland before shifting over to a poster of my favorite podcast, *Crime and Waffles*, and then down to my desk. It's here that I find it—*In the Shadow of a Killer*. Lita Miyamoto's account of catching a notorious local murderer, the Junipero Valley Killer, is both a how-to criminal profiling guide and my favorite book of all time. A calm comes over me as I flip through the well-loved book.

Okay, yeah. I'm a little bit creepy. Here's a handy list of my other "patterns of behavior," as Lita would say:

1) My favorite things to draw are human skulls.

2) While most kids my age are still hooked on *Dog Man*, I read about ghost stories and local murders. Yes, I realize this makes me equal parts creepy and geeky— *creeky?*

3) Since Dad stayed home with me in grade school for weeks at a time (asthma = the WORST), I like hanging out with him more than with most people my own age.

4) I dream of being a criminal profiler. Basically, it's like getting in the heads of bad guys, figuring out how they tick, and catching them. Like a psychological superhero!

5) I observe the people around me and record it in notebooks for data collection. So far, I've filled twenty-two notebooks.

Hmmm. Maybe I'm a *lot* creepy.

All this is probably why I'm two months into seventh grade with only *one* friend. Well, if Shrey is still my friend, that is. He's been weird since that thing last week . . .

"Hey, kiddo." Dad's voice startles me from the doorway.

I swivel to face him. He walks over, sits on the corner of my bed, and takes off his glasses.

OBSERVATIONS:

- Dad keeps looking at me, and then looking away.
- He's cleaning his glasses.

CONCLUSION: He's about to say something difficult.

"Dad, come on." I sigh. "You're doing the glasses-cleaning thing again. How much worse could it get?"

"It's not bad," he insists. "It's a letter—from your mom." He holds out an envelope with my name written in Mom's flowery script, slightly wrinkled from his grasp.

"Not interested," I say, pumping my feet under my chair in an effort to look cucumber-cool. I grab my notebook and start to doodle an unflattering Mom skull with a talking bubble that says *I ♥ yurts!*

"Drew."

I meet his eyes. "Dad. You seriously want me to take that? These letters—this is what she does. Every time she bails on us for one of her adventures or stays with Grandma Joy to 'take a break.' The only difference is that now she's bailing with my counselor, which could make life at school impossible!"

"Sweetheart. You know that Mom and I love you more than anything, right? This isn't about you at all. I hope you know that we love you, and we're *so* proud of the person you're turning into."

I flinch at his use of the word *we*. I know *Dad* loves me. The jury is still out on certain other parents.

None of that needs to be said out loud, though. "I love you too, Dad. Times a *splabillion*," I say, using our made-up word for *infinity*.

Dad cracks the tiniest of smiles, and my chest swells triumphantly. Getting Dad to smile has become my primary goal.

"So. What are you working on today? More of your observations?" Dad changes the subject, unfolding himself from the bed and peering over my shoulder at the notebook.

I consider lying, but the idea makes me tired. "Nah, I was only drawing a picture of Mom. Nothing bad." I give him a cringey smile, holding up the skull picture. "I'm actually thinking of doing a full offender profile on her. You know—like Dr. Miyamoto does."

"Drew . . ." Dad's voice has a warning tone, but it's

way better than the new sad and quiet one he's had all weekend.

"I know, Dad. But I'm reading *In the Shadow of a Killer* again, and I have to practice profiling if I want to be a world-renowned criminologist like Lita. You're the one who named me after Nancy Drew. You had to know I would have an interest in criminal investigation."

"Sure. But you have to admit you go a little far sometimes. Remember Sir Hoppington?"

"What? I *found* that rabbit, didn't I?"

"After interrogating the whole neighborhood and asking everyone to show you their home security cameras," he reminds me. "Look, I won't tell you to stop. Only, try not to think of your mom as a villain. She isn't the Junipero Valley Killer."

I almost retort that Mom has *many* similar traits to the Junipero Valley Killer, but something in Dad's expression stops me. His pale face looks dull and completely drained. Like a vampire sucked out his energy instead of his blood. Is the vampire *me*? Am I being "too much" again?

"I'm gonna lie down for a bit, okay, kiddo?" he says before I can ask. "Come get me in an hour." He kisses my head and shuffles out the door.

It's completely unfair that *Dad* is the one who has to pretend not to cry. When I get sad, I have Dad's shoulder to cry on. He doesn't have a dad anymore—or a mom. They both died when I was little. Mom's family are down in Los Angeles, but that's *Mom's* family. I love Grandma Joy and all my little cousins, but are they still ours? Won't they take Mom's side?

My hands feel sticky with sweat as I set them on my desk, staring absently at the knots in the wood. I focus on a single bead, trickling down, and wonder for a moment if sweat is where tears escape when you don't let them out.

A sudden tightness in my chest tells me that my asthma is about to rear its ugly head if I don't cry soon. But if I can think like a scientist, maybe I won't *feel* at all.

The idea comforts me like a warm, heavy blanket. So I don't cry. Instead, I get to work on my first official profile:

OFFENDER PROFILE

```
NAME: Jennifer Leclair
AGE: 38 RACE: White
```

EYES: ~~Lying~~ Brown **HAIR:** Blond
KNOWN ACCOMPLICES: Mr. Clark, a.k.a.
Liar McPantsonfire

VICTIMS:

1) Sam Leclair, 40: Husband, chocolatier,
awesome dad, all-around good guy.
2) Drew Leclair, 12: Daughter, consumer of
chocolate, true crime enthusiast, usually
awesome.

PRIOR CRIMINAL BEHAVIOR: 1) Disappeared
from 12/2010 to 3/2011. When I was THREE.
2) Bails all the time to "reflect" in
Southern California. Probably goes to
Disneyland without Drew.
MODUS OPERANDI: Usually leaves within
a few weeks of taking a sudden (fake)
interest in "family time" (i.e., buying
me presents, asking about Dad's day,
organizing movie nights).
SIGNATURE: Leaves a handwritten note
signed with "hugs and kisses" even

though she never hugs or kisses me
unless she's leaving.

WEAPONS USED: Fake tears, plane tickets,
absence.

STATUS: At large.

2

I DON'T SEE SHREY until lunch the next day, and part of me wonders if he'll meet me at all. But then I spot him on our usual bench, slumped over a book. We agonized over picking the perfect eating spot all last year, wanting something far enough from the center of the black-top to be quiet, but visible enough for me to make my daily observations. This bench works for both. It's also by the STEM building, which Shrey likes because he has a habit of dropping by his life science teacher's classroom to score peanut-butter cups from the jar on his desk.

When I approach, Shrey's eyes quickly dart away. *Sigh*. This is super weird. Just last week, I felt like we were completely on the same page. TV, movies, video games, eat, repeat. Now, even when I sit next to him, the space between us feels like an impassable void. We aren't just on different pages, we're in completely different *books*.

"Hey," I greet him carefully. My body is starting to actually feel shaky from the tension, so I make my usual mental notes to calm down:

OBSERVATIONS:

- Shrey won't look at me.
- He's tugging at his favorite shirt, an Oakland A's baseball jersey.
- He's rereading *Percy Jackson: The Lightning Thief*, which he only does when he's upset.

CONCLUSION: He's still freaked out about the kissing thing.

I let my gaze fall away from Shrey and start making mental notes about everyone else around us. My Core teacher, Ms. Woodrich, pumps her short legs hurriedly as she stalks across campus. I saw an invitation to a staff luncheon on her bulletin board. Maybe that's today? Johnny Granday is squirting ketchup packets by the cafeteria and laughing when he hits someone. Very common

Granday behavior, unfortunately. Ethan, a boy I know from technology class, is hunched over at the farthest table with his hood pulled down over his face. Almost like he's trying to disappear. It makes sense, since kids have been picking on him for the past few weeks after a nasty post on Instagram. The musical theater kids are practicing a number from *Shrek: The Musical* that seems to involve a giant pink dragon head.

"Uh, how was your weekend?" Shrey fumbles.

I snap back to attention. "Fine. My mom left yesterday." My voice shakes, but I try to keep the statement as offhand as possible. To help my case, I stuff my mouth with a breakfast sandwich. Of course, in the effort to look indifferent, I end up choking and spraying flecks of egg and spinach in Shrey's face.

"Hey!" he protests, wiping a little triangle from his cheek. "I asked for the news, not the . . . uh, sandwich weather."

Swallowing, I say, "Sorry about that. But technically I *did* give you the news."

"That your mom went on vacation?" Shrey gives me a dubious look. "Yeah, that's real breaking news."

I look down at my shoes, reddening as I add, "No, not on vacation. She *left* left. As in forever."

"Wait, *what*? Are you serious?"

"Pretty much." I scan behind us to make sure no one is listening. For a second, I consider adding the Mr. Clark part, but I don't think I'm ready. Maybe I'll tell him later, when we're off campus. Or maybe never.

"You promise you're not messing with me?" he asks, eyes wide.

"Why would I do that?"

Shrey blinks. "Yeah, never mind. Wow. Are you okay?"

Fighting a swell of emotion that sends a dull ache across my belly, I say, "Uh-huh."

"You don't seem okay," Shrey says, which bugs me. Shouldn't I be the leading authority on how I feel?

I'm just about to say that when a loud voice rings out from a few feet away.

"Look at me! I'm talking to YOU."

At the sound of Alicia Alongie's voice, every inch of my body is suddenly paralyzed. Of *course* Alicia would show up and taunt me today. She's the Junipero Valley Killer of our school—murdering people's self-esteem and causing chaos wherever she goes. She's probably figured out that Mom left and wants to torture me.

I whip around to let Alicia know she picked the wrong day, but it's not me she's talking to. My old bully seems to have found a new target—a girl in my class named Trissa.

Alicia sneers. "I'm Trissa! I smell like barf and Doritos!"

Mocking her victims by mimicking them is definitely Alicia's signature, so this isn't a surprise. Although I don't know what the barf and Doritos comment is about.

Trissa's chin is set, like she wants to say something back, but I can also see her lip trembling. She's freaked out. I want to help, but it feels as though my body is sprouting roots that hold me to the bench. Glancing around, I see that everyone looks as shocked as I feel, even though Alicia does this all the time.

Since I can't make myself do anything else, I try to recall everything I know about Trissa. She reads a lot, based on my observations—and the fact that I always see her at the library holds counter. She also speaks up a lot in class. Maybe she's more confident than Alicia's usual targets?

"Barf girl, barf girl!" Alicia chants at Trissa.

"Yeah. I'll go get the blacktop monitor now," Shrey says under his breath. He stands, heading in the direction of two teachers, and then tosses a worried look at me. "Don't say anything, okay?"

Shrey grew six inches in one year and started playing baseball, so he doesn't get picked on much anymore. He always seems nervous, though. Like, any moment, the bullies are going to remember that he's not really a giant, he's just a giant nerd.

I can't let Trissa stand there by herself. I need to say something. My mind racing, I make a quick mental profile of Alicia, trying to piece together what I could say to distract her:

OFFENDER PROFILE

NAME: Alicia Katherine Alongie
AGE: 12 **RACE:** White
EYES: Blue **HAIR:** Blond

RECENT VICTIMS:

1) Drew (a.k.a. me)
2) Trissa
3) That girl in my pre-algebra class with the cute homemade Disney hijabs. Faizah, I think?

SIGNATURE: Takes on exaggerated persona of victim during mocking, observed in at least 75% of incidents.

STATUS: Not suspended for some reason.
KNOWN WEAKNESSES: 1) Carries around a
picture of her dog, Bootsie. 2) Has a
notebook covered with hearts with the
initials I.G. because of her enormous
crush on . . .

Yes! *Isaac Gamez*. All last year, Alicia doodled that guy's name in her notebook, even though he was in eighth grade. I recorded at least six different times she followed him around in my February–May notebooks. There's my opening.

"Hey, Alicia! Can I talk to you?"

Alicia flinches, looking in my direction, but quickly twists her face into an expression of casual disinterest as she saunters toward the bench. Trissa blinks at me, but holds her position.

"Why would *you* want to talk to *me*, Fatface?" Alicia scoffs. "Haven't seen you in a while — since your face deflated or whatever." She laughs as if this were the hottest of hot takes.

Ah, yes. The Fatface period.

Back when my asthma was at its worst, the steroid-based medicine I took caused facial swelling. Yes, it's as attractive as it sounds. For a while, my face was like a big round moon—a siren call to any bully. Alicia is fat, but she's fat *and* pretty. Not me—not back then, at least. On the steroids, I looked like a marshmallow with toothpick limbs, which she loved pointing out.

I give her a fake smile and keep my voice low so that it doesn't shake. "Heh. Good one, Alicia. Anyway, I was wondering. Are you still into Isaac Gamez? Because I actually know him."

"So?" Alicia spits out the word but, in spite of herself, looks at me with sudden interest.

"So, maybe I could help with that. Isaac's a really nice guy. He started working for my dad at the bakery this summer. We spend a *lot* of time together, actually. I could talk you up." I'm *way* playing up my connection to Isaac, but whatever.

Her eyes narrow, and she gives me a disbelieving look, but I can tell I've got her attention. "I don't need help from you getting Isa—"

I cut her off before I can chicken out. "*Or* I could tell him you pick on people for no reason." I pull out my phone and show her a picture I took of Isaac and me at the shop, stacking morning buns. "I mean, if you want, I could tell him that. Or you could stop harassing people. It really is a personal choice, so . . ."

Alicia looks startled, and I almost think she's about to back off when two familiar faces come into view. Ugh. Brie and Emma—Alicia's minions.

They always look smug, but I can't help noticing something more to their expressions today. They wear wicked looks, like snakes after a fresh meal. Emma clasps her cell phone at her hip, one finger linked into a glittery finger strap at the back. Then she shows Alicia her phone while Brie glances at me, snickering.

I can't see what they're looking at, and every instinct tells me to leave, but I can't seem to move. I'm praying that they're watching a sneezing panda or something, when all three of them start laughing.

They're cackling with a tone that rockets me right back to grade school, although I try not to show it.

"Ummmm . . ." I falter.

So, here's the thing. I like to think I have a fairly healthy sense of self-confidence, being awesome and all. But, that confidence came with a lot of effort. And it might not be a hundred percent real. As the girls laugh, a memory worms its way into my head. It was in fourth grade at the height of the Fatface years. I can vividly remember Alicia, Brie, and Emma following me around with a copy of *Ripley's Believe It or Not*, showing me a

photo of a man whose face was grossly puffy and covered in bee stings. *This is you!* they taunted with glee.

The memory cuts me to the bone, but I close my
eyes and force myself to remember Dad's advice: *When
they come at you, don't give them anything to work with,* he
told me after the *Ripley's* incident. *Even if you're dying
inside, pretend that nothing gets to you.*

Using this advice, I came up with my own perfect
method:

DREW LECLAIR'S
THREE-STEP BULLY REMEDY

1) Accept their premise and laugh it off
(like, if someone calls you a name, laugh
right back and agree with them. "Well,
I don't know about *ugly*, but I suppose I
could have brushed my hair today. Thanks
for the feedback, buddy!")
2) Make direct eye contact.
3) NEVER cry.

I finally open my mouth to shut down Alicia and
her friends. But something in the way that *everyone* is

looking at their phones stops me. Are they all watching the same thing? And then staring . . . right at me? The whispers are low, but I can hear them:

Wait, is that her?

The weird girl who draws skulls all the time?

Well, yeah. That *is* me. But why are they talking about it now?

Did her mom really kiss Mr. Clark?

"Call me Dustin" Mr. Clark? Groooosssssss!

Did they really . . . here at school? Where??

I gasp for air like I've been sucker punched. Dad said there was no way anyone knew about that.

As if on cue, Shrey races back with one of the teachers. While Mr. Lee yells at students to put away their phones, Shrey tugs my arm and leads me around the corner of the cafeteria, out of sight.

"Shrey," I sputter, staring back at the crowd. "They're all saying—"

"I know," he interrupts, holding up his phone.

Immediately, I see our unofficial student-run Instagram account, named "Badgers Ahoy!" in honor of our mascot. It's mostly a photo-dump-meets-gossip account, and nobody knows who set it up, but almost everyone follows it. It's racked up even more followers since a troll named Ella Baker Shade started hacking in to post a few weeks ago. Well, the rumor is that they hacked in, at least. One of the eighth-graders who run it could be going rogue.

The latest posts features a picture of me from last year's picture day. My reddish-brown hair is predictably frizzy in the photo, my skin is ghostly pale, and I wear a smile that makes me look like I have no eyes or teeth. Wonderful. In the lower left corner of the photo is an image that I recognize as Ella Baker Shade's usual watermark. I take a deep breath and read the caption:

> Ella Baker Shade is back for more!
> Which EBMS kid's MOM was caught in the staff lounge with Mr. Clark — FULLY making out? Drew Leclair, are you out there? The Shade knows all and SEES all.

My chest clenches like it's in a vise, and I can already hear a faint wheeze escape as I take in the steady gaze of the crowd around me. Because, for the first time, I'm not watching everyone around me. *They're* watching *me*.

3

AN HOUR LATER, I'm staring up at the ceiling in the nurse's office, methodically counting polar bears and beach balls.

Not *actual* polar bears and beach balls, of course. It's the pattern on the office's wallpaper border, and a totally unrealistic one at that. I mean, come *on*. A polar bear would flatten that beach ball in two seconds. Polar bears are jerks. Especially the boy kind, according to a documentary I saw in life science.

"Feeling any better, sweetheart?" Ms. Marika asks me, popping her head in.

Ms. Marika is our attendance clerk, but she's staffing the nurse's station today as usual.

"Yeah. It was probably just my asthma."

She doesn't look convinced. "Your friend Mr. Malhotra said you were upset."

I squeeze my eyes shut. Of *course* I'm upset. And, because my lungs are one big garbage pile sitting in the middle of my chest, the Instagram post propelled me right into a full-blown asthma attack. Thanks, purely ornamental lungs!

"Okay, Drew. Well, the vice principal would like to see you now."

Suppressing a groan, I shuffle down the hall toward Vice Principal Lopez's office. Passing the counseling center, I catch sight of a few familiar faces:

OBSERVATIONS:

- Alicia's would-be victim, Trissa, is sitting in the counseling office lobby reading what appears to be a *Star Wars: Rebels* graphic novel.
- A red-faced Holly Reiss sits next to her, hiding behind her curly hair and fidgeting nervously.
- Ethan Navarez sits in the third chair, with one of his long sleeves pulled down

over what I suspect is a cell phone. He
winces just like Dad does when he loses at
one of his match-and-explode games, which
is probably what Ethan is doing.

CONCLUSION: Could the vice principal be
calling in targets of Ella Baker Shade?
I've only seen posts about Ethan and Holly.
Did I miss a post about Trissa?

Holly is in a bunch of my classes this year, so I noticed when she started to become more withdrawn this
year. Like Ethan (and now me), she was targeted on the
Badgers Instagram. That being said, I've observed her
sitting in the counselor's office a *lot* since school started,
even before the post.

I try to make eye contact with Holly, but she keeps
her face down, layers of curls sweeping over her puffy
eyes. When I lock eyes with Trissa, however, she offers
me a smile and mouths, "Thanks."

"No problem," I whisper back.

Once I sit down in the vice principal's office, Mr.
Lopez says, "So, Ms. Leclair, I've heard from a few of the
other students that there was an incident at lunch." Mr.

Lopez is kind of a mountain. Like Maui from *Moana*, but in a suit and tie. Between this, and his deep voice, everything he says sounds intimidating.

"Um, yeah?" I squeak.

Oof. I hate when I get nervous and end sentences like questions. How would Lita Miyamoto act right now? Would she be nervous, or would she be calm and collected? Definitely the second one. Straightening, I will myself to look like I imagine Lita would in an interrogation room.

"I'll get right to it, Drew. We've been alerted to this Instagram user, Ella Baker Shade, using the 'Badgers Ahoy!' account to bully students. The account was created by students without school permission, and we don't have access. But we're working on figuring out who *does* run the account. Your friend Shreyas let me know that you were the target of a new post today."

"Yes."

"Do you know anything about this post?" Mr. Lopez pivots the screen, which displays a post with a GIF of a gray-faced girl projectile vomiting. I think it might be from an old horror movie that Dad showed me once. Squinting at the text, I read

Ella Baker Shade Alert!

Which seventh-grader spewed Sprite and Doritos all over Mr. Hicks — and the rest of the life science lab class? Trissa Jacobs is our very own . . . *barf girl!*

"Ooohhhhh," I say, with realization. The post is dated Friday, October 18. *That's* why Alicia kept talking about barf and Doritos. Trissa must have been Ella Baker Shade's latest target. Before me, I guess. I was a little busy with Mom drama this weekend, so I missed it.

"We are looking for information *any* student might have about this Ella Baker Shade person, or people."

"I wish I knew," I say. "I saw an eighth-grader logged in to the Badgers account once. Jessica Silva, I think? A few students started it, but anyone could have the password as far as I know. Or the troll could have hacked in."

"Where did you see Jessica logged in to Instagram on campus?" he asks, furrowing his brow. "Our policy is phones turned off bell to bell."

"It was, um, after school," I lie uncomfortably. Most kids find a way to use their phones on the down low, but I'm not going to be the one to blow that secret when I do it too.

"Thank you, Drew. I think that's all," Lopez says,

looking up at me. "You have my word that we will look into this."

"All right."

"I'm very sorry about what you're going through right now," Mr. Lopez says. "With your family, I mean. You can feel free to head back to class now, Drew."

"Um, thanks," I say, even though I'm sorry he brought it up at all.

When I push through the double doors to leave the office, I'm still grumbling to myself, but something stops me. The hairs on my arm stand on end. It's almost as though I can feel eyes on me, but the blacktop is totally empty.

A few stray kids are walking around campus, but it looks like most of them are sixth-graders, tugging self-consciously at their uniforms as they head to PE.

Something in my mind snags on a dirty red set of picnic tables at the far end of campus. It's become a bathroom for our school's seagulls and pigeons. Almost nobody sits over there. So why do I have the feeling, as I walk past the bare, white-streaked table, that someone is watching me from that exact spot?

4

WHEN THE FINAL BELL RINGS, I waste no time before bolting off campus, still shaken from my day at school and the creepy feeling I had after leaving the office. Since Dad's working, I head toward the bakery. A chocolate croissant will definitely make me feel better. Or some marzipan.

Two years ago, Dad opened his own patisserie in Oakland's Dimond district. He named it Leclair's Eclairs (cute, right?), and it's basically my favorite place in the universe, other than Disneyland. All the pastries and chocolate—right at my fingertips.

Today, with the cool air-conditioning on my skin and the rich smell of chocolate from the vats, it might even be *better* than Disneyland. There's also the fact that the whole shop is filled with these little reminders of Dad and me. Our initials adorn the column by the register, the prep room has glow-in-the-dark stars on the ceiling from our trip to the Lawrence Hall of Science, and Dad's office is covered with true crime paraphernalia. Comfort is definitely what I need today, and Leclair's Eclairs is the perfect remedy.

"You look hot," Dad points out as I sling my backpack by his desk. "And a little bit frightening."

I ignore him, but when I duck into the bathroom to wash up, the mirror tells me that he's right. My hair looks like a frizz explosion, my clothes are drenched, and my eyes are bloodshot. "Oh my god . . ." I moan.

I clearly can't tell Dad about what happened today. He'd only worry. But can I hide everything that happened today if it's written all over my hot mess of a face?

Dad steps into the reflection behind me. "I told you," he says with a *tsk* noise.

Removing my hair from its haphazard ponytail, I stomp back into the office and collapse into one of the captain's chairs by his desk. "Maybe I'm hitting my awkward phase," I suggest. "Maybe I'm about to get super gross, and you won't have to worry about me running off with a biker gang."

Dad fixes me with a sympathetic look. "You're not

gross enough to get rejected by a *biker* gang, sweetie. You walked a mile and a half down MacArthur Boulevard in eighty-five-degree heat. It's not a good look on anyone." He rises from his chair and walks toward the kitchen, where his chocolate molds are neatly stacked. From the look of it, he got an order for one billion Pikachu truffles.

"I guess," I mutter, following him. "Hey, did you join the Parent Teacher Organization, by the way? My Core teacher gave me this PTO flyer for you." Reaching into my bag, I root past a few crumpled tests, an overdue library book, and . . . wait. Is that my lunch from last week? It smells like my lunch from last week.

Dad chuckles softly. "Find it yet? Looks like you might find a couple of license plates and half a sea lion in there too."

"Ummm, my backpack is not a dead shark's stomach, and—hey, I'm not *that* messy!"

He snorts. "Yes, you are."

Finally discovering the flyer, I hand it over. "So, PTO?"

Dad's Adam's apple lurches up and down as he swallows nervously. "Yeah, um. I'm trying to make sure all our bases are covered." He busies himself with the chocolate Pikachus (Pikachi? Does it have a plural?) again, but I can tell a cloud has passed over our banter. A cloud named Mom.

"She never even went to the meetings, you know."

"I know, but I've got to start getting out there and making friends again. Other than the occasional lunch with Jervis from Levain Bien, I haven't exactly been social. And I'm sure Wendy and Dan are out now that your mom's . . . um . . . away."

"Whatever. Wendy and Dan are beige anyway."

"Beige?"

"You know. They're *basic*. Whenever they come over, all they talk about is wine and home remodeling. For a while they talked about that boat. They're gonna murder me with boring boat facts someday."

Dad starts to argue, but then looks at me like his mind has been blown. "Wow. You're right. They *are* beige."

"And, besides, you've got me. Sam and Drew against the world, one almond croissant and true crime documentary at a time. Right?"

"Right."

I relent. "Okay, go join the PTO. Make friends. But don't come crying to me when they won't binge watch *Trail of Blood* with you."

He winces. "I probably shouldn't watch that show with you, right? Bad parenting move?"

"You know I'd watch it anyway. But, hey, speaking of your stellar parenting choices, can I go squeeze marzipan into my mouth now?"

With a theatrical sigh, he waves me toward the fridge.

"Woohoo!" I jump up from my captain's chair, open the large stainless steel door to our industrial fridge, and grab a pastry tube.

Eating marzipan is *definitely* worth having a round Ponyo tummy. Even if Mom says that "fat around your middle will kill you." Not all of us can gain weight solely in their butt like Jenn Leclair. Besides, I'm not one of those people that think of *fat* as a bad word. I might have a little chub, but I've learned to *like* my pastry belly, thank you very much.

"Don't ruin your dinner with marzipan," Dad calls, trailing off and muttering about how no father should ever have to say such a thing.

"I won't. Or . . . will I?" I make a cartoonish drooling noise as I squeeze the almond paste into my mouth, pleased that I've managed to steer our conversation back to lighter topics.

Dad looks at me wistfully. "It's nice to have you back around the shop, kiddo. It feels like it's been a while."

I choose not to remind him that I wasn't around for the past two months because Mom insisted on picking me up after school for "mother daughter" time. It was mostly pedicures, spa time, shopping, and "gossip." She'd been stepping it up in the past few weeks, showing up daily with a wink and an iced latte in hand.

You know. Like you do in the days before you abandon your child.

Swallowing the thought, I smile back at Dad. "Hey, if you don't need any more help, can I do my homework in the back?"

He cackles. "I'm sorry, is eating all of my good marzipan *helping*?"

My eyes light up.

OBSERVATIONS:

- Dad is laughing more.
- Dad is teasing me.
- Dad is finally wearing new clothes.

CONCLUSION: He is starting to feel less sad about Mom (so DON'T bring up the Ella Baker Shade thing!).

"Oh, and Drew? I forgot to tell you one thing." He follows me into his office and closes the door behind him. I'm wondering if another glasses-cleaning is coming when he says, "I heard from Mom today."

"Mm-hmmm?"

I'm afraid if I form any words, I'll blurt out that Mom and Mr. Clark are the hot new Ella Baker celebrity couple. Which would both ruin his day *and* my conclusion from a few moments ago.

"She landed safely last night," he tells me, "and she wants you to call before she loses cell signal."

"Of course, Dad," I say with great effort. "I'll do that tonight."

Rage is bubbling inside of me, but I toss him a thumbs-up and wait until the door closes before reacting. Taking my usual deep breaths, I wait for my focus to shift. Fortunately, it works this time.

When I'm finally calm enough, I take out my notebook. After school is the perfect time to record all my observations for the day, and this day was *action packed*. But, just as I put pen to paper and write *Observations*, a shrill ringing breaks through the silence.

"Aaarrghhh!" I yelp, jumping out of my seat.

It's Dad's phone. He must have left it behind—

which isn't unusual, especially when he's dealing with chocolate molds.

My heart skips a beat when I see the caller ID: *Ella Baker Middle School.*

Before I can even think about it, I swipe down to reject the call. Then I wait. Eventually, the little voicemail symbol pops up. Shooting a nervous glance at the office door, I enter Dad's PIN—his and Mom's wedding anniversary—and press Play.

"Hello, this is a message for Sam Leclair. Sam, this is Vice Principal Manuel Lopez from Ella Baker Middle School. I'm calling today to alert you to an issue Drew may be having here at school. Today, during the lunch hour, a social media post was released detailing, er, an issue concerning Mrs. Leclair. I'm concerned that Drew may be upset, and wanted to give you a heads up in case this issue continues. Of course I wish your family all the best—please call me if you have any que—"

"Ahhh!!" I cry, and toss the phone down on the desk.

For another agonizingly long moment, I stare at the phone, unblinking, as if it might explode. Then I pick it back up . . . and press Delete.

5

SINCE THE REST of my Monday was dedicated to obsessing over the deleted voicemail, worrying about Dad, and avoiding looking at the Ella Baker Shade post, I barely slept. This, of course, causes me to wake up late on Tuesday and miss seeing Shrey at the library before school.

When I finally see him at lunch, he doesn't waste any time before shoving his phone in my face. "These are the texts I've sent you since yesterday!" he seethes.

SHREY: What's going on? Someone said Lopez called you into his office. Was it about Ella Baker Shade? You got that asthma attack so fast you didn't even tell me about this Mr. Clark thing. Is it true?

SHREY: Drew. I have tried calling you FIVE times.

SHREY: Six.

SHREY. Seven.

SHREY: I haven't seen you that wheezy in forever. It was scary!

SHREY: DREW. ARE YOU DEAD?

"Where. Have. You. Been?" he asks.

"Okay, you're mad. I get it." I take out my chicken salad sandwich and start pulling off the crust. "I know I haven't told you a lot."

"Um, *understatement!* And I can't believe you didn't tell me about your mom!"

"What? I did yesterday!"

"Not about your mom and . . ." Shrey trails off meaningfully.

Right away, I feel my face flush crimson—the curse of my translucent skin tone. While my day so far hasn't been as bad as yesterday, I've still been hearing hushed tones whenever I walk into a room. Especially when I'm trying to slink by unnoticed.

Look, it's that creepy girl. The one whose mom . . .

Shhhh, she can hear us!

Has she even commented on the post yet? We should tag her until she does.

Honestly, one of the many reasons I haven't been contacting Shrey is because I turned my phone off last night after fifty gazillion Instagram notifications.

"Drew!" Shrey says after I don't respond right away. "Will you talk to me, please?"

Casting a paranoid glance at a group of students nearby, I grab his arm.

"Come with me," I say in a stage whisper, leading Shrey toward the library.

Like I said, I'm an observer. The small garden behind the library is off the main path and provides enough cover to hide us from view, but still allows us to watch students passing by. When we round the corner where the library meets the language arts building, I feel a prickle at the back of my neck. Once again, I feel the heat of someone's eyes on me. Are *we* being watched right now?

Just as we pass the large double doors, I'm sure I see a pair of eyes peering out at us through the glass. Wait . . . is that Trissa Jacobs?

"C'mon," I urge Shrey.

When we've completely hidden ourselves behind a tree, I suck in a deep breath and tell myself, *Keep calm, Leclair. Now is not the time to freak yourself out on top of everything else.*

"All right. So . . . um. What do you want to talk

about?" I ask, hoping he'll switch it up and start gushing about our plan to binge *Avatar: The Last Airbender* over fall break. That boy is obsessed with sky bison. Or maybe Steph Curry. Basketball season is coming up in, like, two months; maybe I could . . .

"Is that stuff about Mr. Clark *true*?" Shrey asks, dashing my hopes.

"Yeahhhhh." I struggle to get the word out, and can feel a wheeze at the back of my throat when I do.

"Wow, that's . . . a lot. Didn't you talk to Mr. Clark a bunch of times this year?" Shrey shakes his head and starts biting at his nails, which he almost *never* does anymore because he's sure his dadi can see him, twenty-five miles away in Fremont. He insists that his grandmother has extrasensory perception and will refuse to make him malai kofta if he even nibbles on a pinky nail. I have to admit, I admire that woman's intimidation techniques.

"I saw him every week for two months," I tell him. "*Mom* asked me to."

Shrey grabs my shoulders, which makes me feel butterflies, but not in a good way. "*Drew*. Why didn't you tell me? I'm your best friend! I could have helped. Remember that time at Eden's birthday party? I totally convinced everyone you were rehearsing for a play."

For one blissful second, I forget everything and

laugh. Of course I remember the birthday party. It was in fourth grade, right as I was getting into true crime and other kids started distancing themselves from me. And then at Eden Dodson's birthday party, while everyone was making craft collars for their furReal friends, all I could talk about was the ghosts of Alcatraz. In particular, an axe-wielding ghost known to flit toward Angel Island at night. In my defense, I was only trying to warn them about murderous ghosts—a public service, really.

"Okay, first of all . . . *fair*," I tell Shrey. "Second of all, I know you're all tall and sporty now, but I don't need your protection! Lita Miyamoto says that girls can take care of themselves." Before I can censor myself, I add, "And third of all . . . are we even best friends anymore?"

Right away, I can see that I've made a mistake. Even though I was half joking, Shrey looks deadly serious. His eyes darken, and he backs up a full step. "*What?*"

"Ummmmm . . ."

My breath immediately catches, and my heart pounds faster. This makes my usual deep breathing a no-go. When I get anxious, it triggers my asthma, and when I get an attack, it feels like I'm breathing through a tiny straw.

So I skip right ahead to part two of my calming technique. I focus on the shrub behind Shrey that looks a lot like *Nerium oleander.* Which can be deadly, especially if ingested. Does the district landscaper know about this?

"Of course we're best friends," Shrey continues after an agonizing pause I've mentally filled with poison plant facts. "Why would you ask me that?"

"I don't know. Because after what happened Friday, it's been weird. You tried to *kiss* me, Shrey. Kissing, as in something boyfriends and girlfriends do—not friends."

There it is. The thing I've been avoiding thinking about since last week. The embarrassed look on his face tells me that he's been trying not to think about it either. It was *so* awkward. We were just hanging out as usual and then suddenly . . . Shrey lips.

"Well, um—" he sputters before I cut him off.

"And then you basically ran off! You didn't return my calls all weekend—"

"*You* didn't return my calls yesterday."

"Because I didn't feel like talking about being totally humiliated!" I shout. I can't help but notice how fast I've gone from zero to upset. Is this the new normal with Shrey? Fighting? Avoiding each other? Willing myself to calm down, I go on. "Shrey, my mom had just left. I thought you didn't want to be friends anymore after the kissing thing. And, guess what, I also found out that the counselor I've been talking to was secretly dating my *mom* the whole time. As in, she was already making out with him or whatever when she *told me to see the school counselor.* So, look. Do you really want to compare lives with me right now?"

Shrey looks away, but says, "You're right. I'm sorry— I really am. And of course we're still friends."

"Best friends?"

He gives me a long and probing look before blurting out the words I never expected to hear: "Do you like guys?"

"Wait, what?"

He shifts awkwardly. "You know what I mean. Is the problem that you don't like *guys*? For kissing, I mean. Or at all?"

Every muscle in my body suddenly vibrates with indignant energy. *Really?*

I try to keep my voice steady, but it shakes on the way out. "So, because I don't want to ruin our friendship, that means I'm automatically gay? Well, guess what, Shrey, I have no idea if I'm gay. I have no desire to kiss *anyone* at the moment." The moment I say it, I realize it's true. Even the idea of kissing seems like a big, wet germ explosion, and I don't want any part of it.

Shrey looks wounded, but reaches a hand out to grab mine. "Drew . . ."

I swat his hand away, and he scowls. "Well, how great can our friendship be if *you* didn't tell me your mom left?"

The words hang between us, heavy and unmovable.

When the late bell rings, he lets out a long sigh. "Okay, if you don't want to talk about it, fine. See you later, then, I guess."

"Later."

As I walk to technology, my whole body jitters as if I've just had a double espresso from Leclair's. Wasn't Shrey supposed to be *comforting* me, with my crumbling life and all?

"Drew!" my technology teacher greets me when I walk into class.

Ms. Tuitasi has this big, booming voice that doesn't match her petite frame. In fact, she might be one of the loudest short people I've ever met. Right now, I find it comforting.

"Hi, Ms. Tuitasi!" I say, ignoring the giggling and stares from Brie and Emma, who are both in technology class with me. "Did you like my paper?"

One of her eyebrows tugs upward. "You mean your *ten pages* on home invaders who strike through neighborhood apps? Very interesting."

Despite all my efforts, I catch a bit of what Emma and Brie are whispering behind us:

Look, there she is! Do you think she's seen the new pic?

God, I would be SO embarrassed . . .

Ugh. Taking a deep breath, I try to focus on Ms. Tuitasi to drown out the noise.

OBSERVATIONS:

• A copy of an incident report lies on her desk, partially hidden. I can't see the name on it, but it's dated in August and labeled *2nd period*. I also catch the words *social media* and *stolen password*.

• Her laptop is open to a tab that reads *Reverse IP lookup*.

CONCLUSION: Maybe Ms. Tuitasi is investigating Ella Baker Shade!

The idea of Ms. Tuitasi as a gritty cyberinvestigator almost distracts me, until a loud hiss from Emma rings out:

"Keep tagging Drew in the new pic!"

Emma's pale face is twisted into a smirk as she stares at me. Brie has the decency to hide behind her glossy black hair to giggle, but the damage is still done. I'm not sure if it's their laughter or the crestfallen look on my face, but Ms. Tuitasi steps forward, facing the class with her eyes ablaze.

"Excuse me!" Ms. Tuitasi bellows, shooting dagger eyes at Brie and Emma. "Are. You. Being. KIND?" It's so intense that, for a moment, I find myself imagining Ms. Tuitasi as Gandalf from *Lord of the Rings*—staring down Alicia's minions and shouting, "YOU SHALL NOT PASS!"

Brie and Emma look like their butts must be sweating from sheer terror as they scramble to pocket their phones.

"Ummmmmm . . ." they say in unison.

"Be better," Ms. Tuitasi says with a stone cold voice. "Or there *will* be consequences."

Despite feeling a tiny lift from the sight of Emma and Brie terrified, I still feel like my feet are glued to the floor at the front of class. *Everyone* is looking at me. Even Ethan, who was the victim of Ella Baker Shade's first post, is staring with a pitying cringe.

My stomach gurgles, cramping up. When it's not my

asthma, it's cramps from my irritable bowel. Oh, no . . .

"Ms. Tuitasi," I say, "can I use the bathroom pass?"

I've barely opened the door to the bathroom before I dig through my bag and reach for my phone. What picture are they talking about?

Once I open my Instagram app, I see it. My insides twist.

Ella Baker Shade has a new post that reads *FOLLOW UP!* It's a screenshot from Facebook, from an account labeled *Dustin Clark*. In the image, Mom and Mr. Clark pose for a selfie, with my mom leaning in to kiss his neck. The caption reads *Getaway with my baby.*

She looks . . . happy.

Hot anger courses through me, and I throw the phone into my bag, reaching instead for the one thing I know will make me feel better: *In the Shadow of a Killer.* When I hold it, I immediately feel calmer—especially as I scan through the familiar table of contents. Let's see, "Keeping the Darkness at Bay," "Nailing Down a Timeline" . . . Is it too much to ask that a book on tracking killers also have a section like "What to Do When Your Mother Leaves and Also Humiliates You"?

My eyes flit over the chapter headings until I see the one that reads "Putting Science First." It doesn't answer my questions about Mom, but it does make me feel immediately calmer to imagine pushing science to the forefront—ahead of my feelings.

In many ways, profiling is as much of an art as it is a science. So it's important to get the science right before the art comes in. Data collection, such as creating timelines and zones and getting the results from the crime scene technicians, is a great first step. Science must come first. Then a profiler can truly analyze all the facts and track down the perpetrator.

Staring at the book in front of me, I ask my go-to question: *What would Lita do?*

Would Lita hide in the bathroom to barf? Would she run and tell Daddy what people have been saying at school? No. She's a scientist. She would assess the situation, remove the obstacle, and protect all potential victims.

Victims like my dad.

I go into my bag again, this time for my notebook. Scanning through my last few months of observations, I see it. I've been watching the behavior of *all* my fellow students since elementary school. I know what they love, what they hate, what makes them tick. Years of obsessing over Dr. Miyamoto have taught me how to construct a good profile. Vice Principal Lopez and Ms. Tuitasi might never find the true identity of Ella Baker Shade. But maybe *I* can.

I can keep Dad from finding out about this, and I can keep this new troll from hurting anyone else—but only if I can figure out who it is.

I need to make some profiles.

6

AFTER SCHOOL, I find myself tucked away behind the science building. The leaf-covered, hidden pathway is another special "alone" spot of mine. Since Shrey probably won't look for me after our fight, I have time to make notes—maybe even an initial profile.

Lita says that science always comes first, but I figure it can't hurt to make a template to start. Data collection and evidence can come later. I review my Mom profile, and the basic one I'd written out for Alicia last night to compare. They're actually not bad. Not FBI-worthy, but decent. Opening my notebook, I write:

OFFENDER PROFILE

NAME: Unknown
AGE: likely 12-13
KNOWN ALIASES: Ella Baker Shade

KNOWN VICTIMS:

1) Ethan Navarez

2) Holly Reiss

3) Trissa Jacobs

4) Drew Leclair

PRIOR CRIMINAL BEHAVIOR: Unknown,
prior to Shade posts. Has been trolling
using the "Badgers Ahoy!" Instagram
(unaffiliated student gossip account) for
approx. two weeks.
MODUS OPERANDI: Posts embarrassing
information relating to Ella Baker
students, along with an image.
SIGNATURE: Hacks the "Badgers Ahoy!"
account and puts a calling card on each
posted image: a manipulated logo of our

mascot, the Ella Baker Badger, wearing a hood and sunglasses. The perpetrator has placed the image on the bottom of each post photo, like a watermark or an artist's signature.

KNOWN CHARACTERISTICS: Look for students who seem to be on the outskirts, or watching their classmates. While posts could be scheduled, organized offenders of this type often like to see their message play out.

WEAPONS USED: Social media, hacking skills (unless the troll is a Badgers moderator), video editing, and maybe design skills for the Ella Baker Shade calling card.

STATUS: At large.

I've barely written the last few words when a noise makes me jerk up, suddenly alert.

"Uhh . . . is someone there?" I call out, remembering the creepy feeling I had yesterday after talking to Mr. Lopez.

Shrey steps into sight. "Hey."

For a second, I'm relieved and don't remember that

I'm *super* mad. When I do, my eyes narrow into slits and my smile becomes an angry scowl.

"Wait!" he cries as I clutch my books and stand. "Before you leave, I want to say I'm *really* sorry."

"*For?*" I ask expectantly.

"For, like, assaulting you with questions," he says in a rush, as if he's expecting me to run away. "For making it about me, okay?"

My jaw, which had been locked reflexively, softens. "Do you really mean it? Because I've got the entire school staring at me, my mom's gone—which, sure, nothing new—but, still, I have to take care of Dad."

"I know." Shrey's eyes are downcast as he kicks at a small pinecone.

"I just don't want to talk about the *kissing* issue right now. Okay?"

"Okay! I mean, yes. I promise I won't bring it up. Seriously."

After giving him a long, searching look, I say, "Okay."

"*Okay* okay?"

"Okay."

"So, can we go back now? Can we just be Drew and Shrey, best friends and also waterbender and airbender, respectively? Because I really don't like this fighting thing . . ."

I shake my head. He looks crestfallen until I say, "I'm definitely a waterbender, but I'd say you're more of a fartbender."

Shrey lets out a tense but relieved laugh. "Now, *that's* fair."

Both of us crack up, and for a split second, it feels like normal again. Of course, now I have to cut short this beautiful moment with the fact that I'm profiling our classmates. But, hey. Shrey knew what he was getting into when he became friends with me.

"Soooooo," I begin.

Shrey blinks. "Oh, man. I know that look. It's the scheme-concocting look. What is it?"

"Well, the short version is that I'm planning to track down Ella Baker Shade using Dr. Miyamoto's profiling techniques."

"Of course you are."

"I'm tired of the bullies at this school getting away with it. Aren't you?"

"Sure. But these mysteries of yours don't always go well. Do I need to remind you about the Exploratorium incident again? You saw the substitute teacher carrying around files on the students and kept asking her if she was a spy!"

"I did *not*."

"Drew. You literally cornered the woman and asked what government she works for. And what about the whole ketchup graffiti investigation last year? You were relentless about handwriting samples. Some people still haven't forgiven you for that."

"It's not about me having friends. It's about *protecting* people, Shrey. I know we can't solve bullying. But Ella Baker Shade is hurting people. We can at least try to stop them."

"They're hurting you too," Shrey points out.

Blinking at him, I sputter, "*Me?* Please, I'm fine. I'm more worried about Dad."

Shrey gives me a funny look, but waves a hand for me to continue.

"But this isn't just about my dad. Did you see how Alicia was with Trissa? And what about Ethan? I mean, people are *still* calling him Pee-than, even though that first post was two weeks ago. And Holly! She's basically been in tears since her post came out. It's not fair. And . . . I know I'm this weirdo and everyone thinks I'm creepy. But maybe a creepy weirdo is exactly who can track this bully down."

Gingerly, I open my notebook and hand it to him, pointing to where I wrote the bare-bones Ella Baker Shade profile.

After a moment of reading, Shrey lets out a snort, and I scorch him with my best Death Star–destroying side eye.

"What? I know it's still rough, but—"

"Drew. It's good," he interrupts. "Well, I mean, it seems good to me. I don't know as much about profiling as you do. It's not that. Uh. How do I say this? The profile reminds me of *you*. Not the mean stuff, but the part about watching people."

I grab the notebook, scanning down. "Okay, fine. It does sound a *little bit* like me in that section. But obviously it's *not* me, and . . . You know what? Actually, that's perfect!"

"Yeah?"

"Yeah! Lita says that sometimes you have to put yourself in the mind of a criminal and see things from their point of view. Maybe I *am* uniquely qualified to find this guy."

"Or girl!" Shrey points out.

"True! Way to be a feminist, buddy."

"I try. So, we're figuring out who Ella Baker Shade is. Because—let me get this straight—if we catch this one person and they're punished, it might make people more scared to be bullies?"

"Basically. Are you in?"

Shrey smiles. "I'm in."

A sudden crackle of dry leaves makes both of us jump. I spin my head each way, scanning our surroundings.

"What was that?" Shrey whispers.

"I don't kn . . ." I trail off as I see none other than Trissa Jacobs rounding the corner of the STEM building.

"Umm . . . sorry to interrupt," she says.

OBSERVATIONS:

- Trissa is looking back and forth between us.
- Her body language shows hesitation and protection (crossed arms, gripping backpack straps, one foot digging into the ground).
- She is "sorry to interrupt."

CONCLUSION: She heard *everything* we said. Maybe even what I said about the kissing thing.

"Oh, hey, Trissa!" I hurry to cover. "We're just here, being casual and talking about . . . regular, uhhh . . ."

"I heard you," she says, looking between us. "About Ella Baker Shade. I heard you, and I want in."

"Wait, what?" I stop trading agonized looks with Shrey and turn back to Trissa with surprise.

She fidgets with her hands, looking as though she's preparing for a speech. "Well, I've been wanting to talk to you since yesterday and ask how you knew that stuff about Alicia and Isaac. I thought maybe you'd have some tips for the next time she comes after me—at least until this 'barf girl' thing dies down. Anyway . . . I kind of followed you." She twirls the tip of her shoe into the ground again, and then seems to think better of it, wiping it on her pants leg. "I didn't mean to eavesdrop; I just want to help."

So Trissa *has* been watching me!

Shrey is completely facepalming, so I try to keep it together for the both of us. "Okay, you heard Shrey and me talking—"

"Do you really think you can find Ella Baker Shade?" Trissa rushes to ask. "I mean . . . I hear you, like, *know* stuff about people. Is that true?"

Do I tell her the truth—that I like to solve cases and

make notes on kids' behaviors in my notebooks? Seems like a bad idea. Like, a get-me-kicked-out-of-birthday-parties idea. But, then again . . . Trissa probably wants to see the Shade caught as much as I do.

"Maybe I know *some* things about people."

"Drew!" Shrey protests. Which is fair. I mean, he's only recently gotten past being bullied at Cypress Grove Elementary. How is he supposed to trust this girl we barely know? I try to communicate to Shrey with a look that I'm fishing for more information.

"Look," Trissa goes on. "I'm not trying to mess with your plan. I just want in. Since the whole barf thing in August, kids have been pretty awful. Nobody seems to remember the fact that the *reason* I threw up was because we were dissecting a cow eye and Johnny Granday kept yelling that the cow's eye had moved and was staring at me."

"That's messed up," I say, shaking my head.

"Right? I told the teacher, but of course nothing happened to Johnny. He was being *super* nasty, too. The teacher just kind of laughed it off and gave me a pass to the nurse. Probably doesn't hurt that Johnny is white. Just saying."

Shrey nods. "You're right. If you had come back at

him, *you* probably would have been the one to get in trouble."

"Yep," Trissa agrees. "I know they don't mean to, but I always feel like teachers are eyeballing me. And my friend Liz is always getting called out for disrespect when Alicia Alongie gets away with everything. It's so weird."

"I recently made a pie chart on Ella Baker suspension rates by race," I say with a nod. "The uneven percentages are *super* incriminating."

Trissa laughs. "You're . . . kind of strange, aren't you?" Something in her open expression tells me she doesn't think that's a bad thing.

"Well, yeah. You've probably heard about the skull thing."

"Sure. But I figured you were goth or something."

"No, I'm . . . my own kind of weird."

"I can dig it, Skull Girl," she says with a warm smile. Then she claps her hands together. It's a call to attention, and I half expect her to say something teachery, like *one, two, three, eyes on me!* "So, are we doing this? Finding Ella Baker Shade, I mean. How would we start?"

I glance over at Shrey, then back at Trissa. How do I know we can trust her?

After the Alicia incident, I reviewed my notes on her

from the past year. I have to admit, she came out looking pretty good. Trissa is a member of the "Random Acts of Kindness" club, where kids place encouraging notes all over school for students to find. Her body language is soft and open, very unlike your average bully body language. I recorded one time when Trissa gave a kid her sandwich last month when he forgot his lunch. All my evidence points to Trissa Jacobs being *super* nice.

But how can I be sure she's not Ella Baker Shade? After all, Lita Miyamoto says that perpetrators try to insert themselves into an investigation by offering to help. Could that be what Trissa's doing? On the other hand, why would Trissa be posting about herself?

"All right," I say after a moment's debate. I reach forward to shake Trissa's hand while Shrey looks on dubiously. "You're in."

7

A FEW HOURS LATER I find myself at home, unraveling a large ball of red yarn and staring at my desk thoughtfully. Why? Because, after reviewing my profiles and consuming four powdered cappuccinos, I've decided to go full crime board. Lita says that it's the best way to organize timelines and evidence while you're tracking leads. And, I mean, it's a *crime board*. How could I not? The whole concept brings to mind a seasoned investigator pinning up pictures, marked-up maps, and recorded leads until they finally nail the perpetrator. Which could be *us* if we find Ella Baker Shade!

I would have waited for Shrey and Trissa, but two things stopped me. First, it might be too soon for a potential new friend like Trissa to see Crime Board Drew. And, Shrey? Well, I'm pretty sure he thinks my obsession is getting a little old. Or "babyish," which he said once and makes *no* sense. How is solving crimes *babyish*?

He can say that to my face when we catch Ella Baker Shade.

First, I write a list of the five suspects. Obviously, Johnny Granday and Alicia are on the list, as they are the worst serial offenders on campus. But I also have quite a few notes on Brie and Emma, along with this awful boy named Micah who just started at Ella Baker this year. When I'm done, I pin the list to the center of my board.

PERSONS OF INTEREST

1) ALICIA KATHERINE ALONGIE

MEANS: Has access to Instagram on campus computers and cell phones, and got A's in technology class all last year.
MOTIVE: Alicia has been teasing kids since grade school, and seems to take extra satisfaction in making kids cry.

Cyberbullying could be a next level for her.

OPPORTUNITY: Was with me on the blacktop when the video posted, but could have scheduled the post.

COUNTERPOINT: Alicia likes to look her victims in the eye when she targets them so she can see them get upset. Would anonymous bullying be her style?

2) JONATHAN EMILIANO GRANDAY

MEANS: Has access to Instagram like Alicia and everyone else. No indication of any advanced tech skills, however.

MOTIVE: Johnny loves to be part of the action when anyone is being laughed at. Like when he taunted Trissa until she got sick. Could this need to torment people be escalating?

OPPORTUNITY: Was spotted on the blacktop at the beginning of lunch.

COUNTERPOINT: Johnny likes to pick on people in person and laugh at his own mean jokes. Would he change his method this easily?

3) BRIE TERESA COLLINS

MEANS: Has access to Instagram like everyone else. Brie submitted graphic designs in last year's "Reflections" yearbook contest, so she has tech skills.

MOTIVE: Previous notes conclude that Brie has an attention-seeking personality. Revealing gossip and teasing may make her feel important.

OPPORTUNITY: Could have scheduled the post in advance.

COUNTERPOINT: Brie is more of a follower. Is it likely she would be the mastermind, or could she be doing Alicia's bidding?

4) EMMA MARIN CRUZ

MEANS: Has access to Instagram like everyone else. However, she loudly complained about her D grade on Ms. Tuitasi's first technology assignment of the year.

MOTIVE: Seems obsessed with keeping Alicia's favor. Could she be doing this to impress her?

OPPORTUNITY: Could have scheduled the post in advance.

COUNTERPOINT: Emma has an active presence on social media, in which she frequently makes negative comments on people's photos. Would she feel the need to create a separate anonymous account?

5) MICAH (MIDDLE NAME?) DEMMERS

MEANS: Has access to Instagram on campus computers and cell phones. However, Micah is new enough that more data is needed on whether he's a regular user.

MOTIVE: A proven desire to humiliate others.

OPPORTUNITY: Was nowhere to be seen during the reveal of the post about Mom and Mr. Clark.

COUNTERPOINT: Micah's signature seems to

be mocking people for their appearance.
This has not been witnessed online.
Investigate possible fake handle.

Staring at the board, I let out a long "hmmmm . . ." The suspect list sits alone in the center of the board, devoid of a theme so far. So I put on some classical music (because all detectives solve crimes to classical music; haven't you heard?) and flip through *In the Shadow of a Killer* again to narrow my focus.

According to Lita, "geographic profiling" is one of the best tools for a profiler. It's basically making a map of crime scenes to see if there is a pattern. Deciding to give it a try, I break out my artist's notebook and make a quick sketch of the school from a bird's-eye view, including each building and the paths connecting them. Next, I bust out the multicolor pens, because everything is better with color coding.

I use a different color for each suspect on the map, and tack down short lengths of red yarn to track their locations during the target time. Since the only target time I'm aware of is the Ella Baker Shade reveal at lunchtime yesterday, the pattern is pretty simple so far. Alicia, Brie, and Emma were all near me just after the post went live, while Johnny Granday had been in sight by the cafeteria. Micah Demmers wasn't on the blacktop that I'd seen, so the small yellow dot I created for him has a penciled-in question mark to the side of the board.

My next tool is victimology, which may sound like a made-up word, but it's totally real! Victimology is the study of what kind of victims a criminal has, but I'll bet it can work just as well on a bully. After all, murderers are, like, *next-level* bullies. Lita Miyamoto used victimology to study the Junipero Valley Killer's victims. But she also used it to catch a notorious thief, the Masterpiece Man, who targeted museums on the New England seaboard a few years ago. *A criminal's chosen target*, Lita says, *is a part of them.*

Unfortunately, I still don't have a connection other than the fact that the four victims are all in seventh grade at Ella Baker. I can't find anything more meaningful—even after checking a year's worth of notebooks for observations on Ethan, Trissa, and Holly.

Sensing a dip in momentum, I shake it off and get back to work on my suspect list. My lists, of course, require *more* colored pens. By the time I'm finished, my eye has a twitch, and a glance in the mirror tells me that my transformation into "mad scientist" is complete. Since Dad is due home soon (and the last thing I need is him catching me profiling for real), I tuck the partially complete board under my bed and open my notebook to continue the work.

So far, a main suspect is emerging: Alicia Alongie. Brie and Emma don't strike me as the types to break out on their own. And, despite his rap sheet, Johnny isn't observant enough to be Ella Baker Shade. Maybe it could be Micah—especially since he started this year. But I'll need a lot more data to move him to the top of the list. I briefly consider that it could be someone from sixth or eighth grade, but then why would all of the victims be in seventh? Alicia is the only one that checks every box of the initial profile. And, if that incident report on Ms. Tuitasi's desk *is* important, Alicia is in her second period class. Maybe she was the one who got caught stealing passwords.

But am I trying too hard to fit my profile to the suspect, like Lita warned? Am I putting science second? I also have to consider that I might want Alicia to be Ella Baker Shade because of the Fatface years.

I squeeze my eyes shut, momentarily thrust back to third grade, when my asthma had worsened to the point where I had to go to the hospital for pneumonia three times in one year. Sometimes, Alicia would go so far as to take unflattering pictures of me when I was at my sickest to torture me with later. That kind of thinking definitely makes her an organized offender—someone who plans their crimes before the fact.

"Highly organized," I murmur. "That fits."

"What fits?" a voice says from my doorway. I practically fall off the bed, and Dad comes rushing over to steady me. "Whoa, honey. Didn't mean to scare you."

"You didn't *scare* me. You surprised me," I correct him. "Can I help you?"

He gives me a funny look. "Can I *help* you? Is that how we're communicating now? Do I need to find a parenting book on how to deal with my newly snide tween?"

Immediately softening, I say, "Sorry, Dad. I'm just focused."

"What are you doing? Still profiling your mother?"

"I'm working on my profiling, yes," I say carefully. *Not* lying, but still close enough that sweat prickles at the palms of my hands.

"All right. But remember you actually need to *call* Mom. She and her, um, *friend* are finishing up in Poipu and are heading for the east shore to—"

"Mmm-hmmm," I mutter, hoping he'll stop talking.

"Also, Grandma Joy and Aunt Lucy both called yesterday."

"I'll call everyone back soon, okay?" I huff. Then,

seeing his face, I add in a softer voice, "Are we doing our Murder and Mayhem night?"

Dad purses his lips as if he wants to say more, but lets it go. "Of course, sweetie. We're carbed up and ready to go."

"Did you get a batard from Levain Bien?" Dad makes his own pastries and chocolates, but Levain Bien is the bakery's bread distributor.

"Oui."

I immediately start drooling and tent my hands with glee. "Excellent. Bust out the olive oil and vinegar. You know, we can eat in front of the TV now, right? Mom's not here . . ."

He gives me a sad-excited smile that breaks my heart. "Let's do it!"

Ever since Dad gave up on shielding me from watching what Mom deemed "inappropriate media," we've been having Murder and Mayhem nights. It includes everything from true crime documentaries to procedurals to horror films. Sometimes we even sneak in Halloween episodes from *The Simpsons* if Dad's nostalgia kicks in.

Making my way down the long hallway to the front of our house, I purposefully avoid looking at the photos lining the walls: hiking with Mom and Dad at Redwood Regional, a JCPenney portrait of Mom holding me as a baby, and a picture of us dressed up for Halloween in a family costume. We were the Incredibles—with Mom and Dad as Bob and Helen Parr and me as Violet.

How long before Mom and Mr. Clark have their own hallway in a new house, with a rebooted family and their own JCPenney portraits?

Nope. Eyes forward, Leclair. Straight ahead.

"I decided to make panzanella!" Dad announces when I walk into the kitchen.

Panzanella sounds awesome, but my mind is still fixed on the hallway of lies behind me. I take a deep breath. "Hey, Dad? When can we take down the pictures of Mom?"

His eyes pop. "Uh, why would you want to do that?"

I busy my hands by tearing off a piece of batard and shoving it in my face.

"Drew . . ."

"Wufff?"

"Seriously? You cannot stuff your mouth with carbs every time you don't want to talk about something."

I force the bread down my throat. "Why? *You* do that."

He kinda side-eyes me, but then says, "Yeah, okay. That's fair. But do we need to talk about this? I want to talk, but I also don't want to push."

"I don't want to talk about it. But I do want to take down the pictures. At least for now, all right?" My voice cracks annoyingly as I add, "I can't look at her face right now. The whole hallway feels like a work of fiction, not our family. I can't stand it."

Dad looks beaten. "All right. Which pictures?"

"Everything that's not in your room."

"Okay." Dad nods, and I rip another piece of batard and offer it to him.

"Bread with your bread?"

"Nothing better as a side dish to a bread salad than a big hunk of bread." Dad sweeps a hand toward the couch, where *Trail of Blood* is already queued up on the screen. "Shall we?"

"We shall."

Smiles have been rare these past few days, but a happy one spreads over my face. It feels good. While Dad busies himself mixing the panzanella and filling ramekins with olive oil and balsamic vinegar, I collapse onto the couch.

A melodic *bling!* rings out from my phone, and I suppress a groan. It sounds like a notification, not a text. Have kids started tagging me on the picture again? I screw up my face in confusion when I see it's a new post.

"Yikes. That was fast." Bracing myself, I read:

Check out this video of "pitch perfect" Connor Brady, rehearsing for the musical. Looks like someone's voice is changing. Maybe the program will read SQUEAKER in the role of Shrek. You can run but you can't hide from ELLA BAKER SHADE!

Dad finally sits next to me on the couch, starting the show. Usually, my excitement over *Trail of Blood* would outweigh any case. But, I can't help but think that now I have my *own* victims to deal with. And it might be time to talk to them.

8

THE FIRST THINGS I notice after I stumble out of bed this morning are the wooden-framed pictures on the mantel. They used to hold pictures of me and Mom walking on the Golden Gate Bridge and posing on Crissy Field below. Now every frame is a selfie that Dad and I took the night before, gorging on bread and posing in front of the *Trail of Blood* logo on the TV. I grab a bowl of Choco-Crispers and start to slurp them up. After a moment, I pick up the bowl and walk around, curious to see if he's changed any more pictures.

Wow. He has. *All* of them.

Every picture is of Dad and me. Like the time we stayed out till midnight filling our bellies with choco-late-dipped churros. Or the time we waited in line for an hour to buy a limited edition Poe Dameron figure at the comic book store. A warm feeling bubbles up inside of me, and I find myself smiling until my cheeks feel tight. He must have stayed up *half the night* printing photos.

Just like that, my house feels like a home again.

"Hey, kiddo," a voice sounds from behind me. "You're up early."

"And you slept in," I counter. "Should I walk to school today, or are you dropping me?"

"I'll drop you. So . . ." He trails off, looking at me hopefully.

"Thanks, Dad. I mean it. I love it."

"This doesn't mean anything, you know. Your mom is not out of our lives. It might be the end of our marriage, but it doesn't mean . . ."

"I get it." Pushing down the thought of Mom and Mr. Clark, off making their own memories, I take a deep breath. "I do. Thanks."

"You're welcome." He gazes down at the row of hallway pictures. "Did I go *too* nerdy?"

"Uh, yeah, Dad. You went too nerdy. But that's us, right?"

Since Dad was the one staying home with me during the asthma bouts, he often worked from home while showing me his favorite shows. Turns out, binge watching is the *best* when you can't breathe. Way better than being outside in a sea of allergens, that's for sure.

"It's perfect," I say, dodging one of his aggressive hair-tousles. "Really, Dad."

Dad heads for the master bedroom, and the dull white noise of the shower immediately sounds through the walls. Glancing at the clock, I realize I have a few minutes before getting dressed in my "not a uniform" uniform (the dress code is pretty strict at Ella Baker). With my extra time, I update the victim list to add Connor and snap a picture of the crime board to show Shrey and Trissa. I notice as I pack up my backpack that Dad's "picture project" has already made me feel lighter. That, along with the pride I'm feeling over my crime board, makes me think, *Maybe today won't be so bad after all.*

***

I'm not totally wrong. The whispers about me, which were going strong yesterday after Ella Baker Shade's follow-up post, are finally dying down. Unfortunately, that comes at the expense of Connor Brady. Although the whole Squeaker thing doesn't seem that bad, I notice Connor looking downcast between classes. Which, of course, makes me feel awful for my relief at being out of the spotlight.

Still, I'm excited as I head for lunch, when I can show Shrey and Trissa my work. But as I dodge past students to make my way to the library, I slam right into someone.

"Oof!" I exclaim, rubbing my shoulder.

When I look up to see what mountain I just ran into, I see my second-least-favorite person and second-*most*-favorite suspect. Johnny Granday.

"Hey, Leclair. Too busy thinking 'bout Mr. Clark slipping your mom the tongue to walk straight?" He lets out a loud guffaw and gestures broadly, smacking a passing student I realize is Ethan (a.k.a. victim #1). Ethan rubs his arm, but keeps moving. I don't blame him. Despite the fact that the phrase "slip the tongue" brings a fresh splash of bile up my throat, I keep my cool and use my bully remedy. Eye contact, agree, don't cry.

"You got me!" I say brightly. "I'm also thinking about pizza, so if you'll excuse me . . ."

Predictably, Johnny is too dense to process my words until I've already moved past him and ducked into the library. Before I head toward my secret spot, I take a few deep breaths. The last thing I want to do is distract from our first official meeting with Johnny Granday drama. My eyes follow the READ posters around the room until I land on one that says READING IS DEVIOUS, which has a pattern I can focus on. After a few seconds, I feel ready to find Trissa and Shrey.

"Hey, Drew!" Trissa beckons in a stage whisper from the 800s alcove of the library when I round the corner. She's not exactly being covert, and there are a few other things I notice off the bat:

OBSERVATIONS:

```
• Trissa has her usual braids, but she's
added a cascading rainbow of green, blue,
and red rubber bands.
• Her solid-color Tom's shoes have been
replaced by a pair that features the sig-
nature pattern of R2-D2.
• She's wearing one of those flip sequin
shirts with what looks like a Yoda shape.


CONCLUSION: . . .
```

"Having a Star Wars day?" I drop my backpack and sit cross-legged in the corner of the stacks. Since I'm nice, I don't point out that she's wearing the most conspicuous outfit possible.

Trissa shrugs. "Well, yeah. What can I say? I'm a fashion Jedi, and I love finding ways to keep my style, even with the dress code." She waves a hand across her outfit. "See—I can wear my uniform shirt over this and there's nothing in the code about red and blue on *shoes*. Besides, I love Yoda."

"Yeah, me too," I admit. "You don't get any flak when you take off your sweatshirt?"

"Nope. At least, not in the library," Trissa tells me. "Mr. Covacha is cool. That's why I pretty much live here. Well, that and the books."

"Mr. Covacha *is* cool," I agree, looking over at our school librarian.

Young and often found wearing pop-culture-themed Hawaiian shirts, Mr. Covacha is the polar opposite of your stereotypical shushing librarian. He's always holding comedy and music events in the library, and he never tells us to quiet down unless we're *really* pushing the boundaries. Which, admittedly, happens. Mr. Covacha also buys teen and adult titles for the library and actually lets us check them out. As he says, *I'll give you a content warning and ask if your parents are okay with it. But, as a librarian, I am honor bound not to keep information out of the hands of curious youth.*

I love the idea of being honor bound to do something. If I ever do get to the FBI Academy, I wonder if there'll be an oath. What am I thinking? There will *totally* be an oath!

"So, Skull Girl." Trissa interrupts my fantasy. "What have we got?"

I glance around, craning my neck to see if I can spot Shrey. "Where is he?" I mutter. Pulling out my phone, I check for texts.

SHREY: Mr. Garrison wanted to talk to me after algebra. Start without me — you can catch me up.
SHREY: Also, I read a rumor during Tuitasi's class that a new Paper Mario is coming for the Switch. COUNT BLECK!!! COUNT BLEEECCCKKKK!

Letting out a relieved laugh, I put down my phone. Shrey and I spent months on Super Paper Mario last year. Maybe he's finally getting back to *non*-kissing topics. That would be nice.

"Is he coming?" Trissa asks.

"Yeah, but he's running late," I tell her. "He says we can get started, though. Here's what I have so far."

I show her the picture of my crime board. "You see, the yarn points to both suspect locations during the last post *and* the victim they might have a motive to target!"

I'm rattling on excitedly, but something in her dazed expression tells me to pull back a bit. I've seen that look before.

"All right," Trissa says as she hands back my phone and looks at me carefully. "So you're, like, *into* into this stuff."

"Yes," I say with a sigh. "That's me. Creepy with a capital C."

"No, that's not what I meant! I just . . . This is very thorough."

"Um, thanks?"

She rests a hand on my shoulder and smiles. "I mean it as a compliment. I swear."

"Oh, okay. Thanks!" I say, my heart lightening.

"I do have a few questions, though." Trissa points at the crime board photo on my phone. "First: What is profiling, exactly? Like, how does it help?"

"It's just a way to track criminals. Mostly murderers, but not exclusively," I say, bubbling with excitement that I'm actually being *asked* this question. "We assess the psychological traits of a suspect to see if they may have committed the crime. For this case, we study the kids at school to see if they could be capable of being Ella Baker Shade. Then we make a profile."

"Got it. Sort of. And what's victimology?"

I explain the definition of victimology, along with the history of the National Crime Victimization Survey—which she didn't ask for, but whatever.

"All right, cool," she says as I finish up.

I dig my notebook out of my bag, handing it to her. "Here," I say. "I also copied down the list of suspects if you want to see it closer."

She peers down, and I can tell she's jumped right to the Johnny Granday section from where she places her finger. "Thanks for this," she says, pointing at the section where I made it clear that Johnny caused the vomiting incident that led to the Shade's post on Trissa.

"It's the truth, right?" I say, shrugging and shifting uncomfortably on the nubby carpet. Even though I don't want to, I'm still feeling shaken from my brief run-in with Johnny in the hall. "And I didn't just get it from you. I actually remember Mr. Hicks talking about it in the staff room last month."

Trissa blinks at me. "Why were *you* in the staff room?"

"I'm a teacher's assistant for the office during third period. Ms. Marika has me staple newsletters and stuff in the staff room because there's more space. I guess you could say I tend to blend into the background. The teachers don't notice me, and they say all *sorts* of interesting stuff. And leave papers lying around."

"So, you're some kind of spy?"

"Well, not really. More like a *detective* . . ." I trail off, imagining myself in a Sherlock Holmes cap.

"Anyway," Trissa continues, fiddling with one colorful braid. "A lot of people at this school don't seem to care about the truth at all."

"*I* care. The truth is, like, my number one favorite thing!"

"Sounds serious," Trissa says with a sly grin. "Are you and 'the truth' getting married? And, more importantly, am I invited to the wedding?"

"Whose wedding?" Shrey sits down and looks at us expectantly.

"Truth and justice," Trissa says, looking at me wickedly. "Drew's passionate loves."

"What?"

Shrey looks confused already, so we catch him up on what he missed. He lets out an amused snort when he sees my crime board, but I choose to ignore him.

"Now that Shrey is here, we need to figure out what's next," I say. "Especially with Ella Baker Shade's new post last night."

"Agreed," Trissa says. "Poor Connor."

"We could question our suspects first," I suggest.

"No!" both Shrey and Trissa shout in unison.

Mr. Covacha peers in our direction. I give him a little wave and then lower my voice, hoping the others will follow my lead. "Okay, we'll talk to the victims first—Ethan, Connor, and Holly. But then we have to talk to the suspects. Lita says that data collection is step one in any investigation."

"Wait, Lita? Who's Lita?" Trissa hisses.

"Oh, that's Dr. Lita Miyamoto," Shrey informs her. "One of the top criminal profilers in the country, which I've heard a thousand times. She's basically Drew's hero."

"Not basically. *Is*."

"Okay, she *is* Drew's hero." Shrey rolls his eyes and starts to dig around in my backpack.

"Hey!" I protest.

"Why do you have a large ball of yarn in here? Oh, yeah. Your crime board. Anyway," he says when he pulls out *In the Shadow of a Killer*, "Lita Miyamoto caught the Masterpiece Man *and* the Junipero Valley Killer."

"The who and the *who?*"

I squeeze my eyes shut, summoning all my willpower not to scream. "The Junipero Valley Killer," I say in a measured voice, "is only the most nefarious murderer that the Bay Area has seen in the last thirty years. You haven't . . . I mean, the *news* at least?"

Trissa shrugs. "My parents and I don't really watch the news. Dad says it's too depressing."

"Anywhoos," I say, trying not to facepalm. "Lita is the authority on capturing serial offenders like Ella Baker Shade."

I hope that bringing us back to the task at hand will refocus them, but then Trissa says, "Serial . . . offender?"

Shrey and Trissa share a look.

Trissa puts one finger to her chin in an exaggerated thinking pose. "Now that I think about it, what's *murder*? I've never heard that word."

They crack up. I regard them both through slitted eyes for a moment, until I can't take it anymore and I crack up, too. They may be annoying me, but I'm also starting to feel something else—something warm and light from deep inside that makes me wonder: is this what it feels like to have friends, *plural*?

Because I kind of like it.

9

VICTIM PROFILE

NAME: Ethan Victor Navarez

AGE: 12 **RACE:** Latinx

EYES: Hazel **HAIR:** Black

KNOWN HOBBIES: Coding and graphic
art. Won the "Ella Baker Reflections"
contest in sixth grade for designing
the yearbook cover. Coding is an
assumed hobby, based on the fact that I
overheard Ms. Tuitasi asking him to work
on this year's "Hour of Code" event.

~~Crime~~ **OFFENSE COMMITTED AGAINST VICTIM:**
Ethan Navarez was the first known victim

of Ella Baker Shade. A Ralph Wiggum
pants-wetting image was used as the
cover photo, bringing back an old rumor
that Ethan wet his pants during a spirit
assembly. Ethan has been called Pee-than
ever since.

"So, Ethan," I say, sliding into the empty chair beside
him and panting slightly. I'm trying my best to look calm
and composed. Like I didn't just wheeze up a flight of
stairs to get here. "You started at Cypress Grove Elementary in fifth grade, correct?"

Ethan knits his brow in confusion and glances
around. "Um, me?"

"Yes." I say, trying my best to channel a seasoned
detective. Picture Sherlock Holmes, but in sweatpants
and a color-neutral polo. "That's right. You were in Mr.
Pike's class, right? I was with Mrs. Garcia."

"Yeah, I was in Mr. Pike's class." He's still looking
over his shoulder as if he's not sure I'm really talking to
him. Or like he thinks a camera might pop out at any
second.

Taking in Ethan's body language, I wonder if I'm using the wrong tack. Lita says that victims are the most

overlooked factor of an investigation, and often have details that a traditional investigation will miss. But Shrey and Trissa said that we need to be gentle when questioning Ella Baker Shade victims.

"The last thing we need is to be going around like cops, scaring people who are already scared," Trissa had pointed out.

The nervous look on Ethan's face tells me she might be right.

"Sorry." I take a deep breath, summoning all of my "regular girl" energy. "It's just—you know, *both* of us were targeted by this Ella Baker Shade troll. I guess I'm trying to figure out why. What is it about us?"

"Ohhhh." Ethan's face relaxes. "Yeah. Look, I don't know why they posted that thing about me. But, to be honest, kids called me Pee-than before that post. Johnny Granday, like, ninety-nine percent of the time. He came up with it. Not too clever, but you know how it is."

Students have started to file into technology class, including Brie and Emma, who are still eye-stalking me constantly. So I lower my voice as I ask, "Has Johnny Granday been targ—er, *mean* to you since you started here?"

He shrugs, and follows suit by lowering his own voice. "Since Cypress Grove, actually. I'm small and smart, and he's a *giant* and not smart. Seems like he goes after people like me."

"That's true." Letting my eyes flit over to my notebook, it takes every ounce of my willpower not to write this down. That's *two* of our victims who were regularly bullied by Johnny Granday. "Umm, do you have any idea who could have posted that?"

"I mean, probably Granday? He's literally the worst. It's like he thinks everyone is a joke."

"Could be," I say noncommittally. "But there's also Alicia Alongie, Micah Demmers—"

"Okay, class!" Ms. Tuitasi announces, clapping her hands together. Today, she's wearing a purple cardigan that matches her hair. When I squint, I see that the sweater has HTML code printed across the body and arms. Which is *pure* Ms. Tuitasi. "Let's take two minutes to settle in," she says loudly, "and then we'll watch the rest of our documentary. Remember, we're losing a few days of class for Fall Fest and October break. Let's use that time to select new project topics."

Ethan moves to empty his backpack, and I notice a few things:

OBSERVATIONS:

• He is wearing a T-shirt that has a picture of a shark eating a computer that reads JUNIPERO VALLEY WHITE HATS.

• The margins of his notebook are filled with a string of cartoons of spiders in old-fashioned top hats.

CONCLUSION: Ethan has some kind of hat obsession? I've never seen him wear a hat. Weird.

"Okay, Ethan," I say, staring at the jaunty spiders. "Thanks for talking to me."

He gives me an eager smile. "No problem. Let me know if you find anything out. I'd *love* to see Granday finally nailed for something, y'know?"

"Trust me," I say, turning back to face the projector screen. "I know."

I sneak my phone out and text Trissa.

DREW: Hey. Talked to Ethan N. and he thinks it's Granday.

TRISSA: Honestly I do too. That boy is the WORST.

DREW: 😵 I dunno. I still think he's not smart enough to pull off this stalker cybertroll thing.

TRISSA: Ok that's fair.

DREW: Still up for more questioning after school? After that, we can meet at my super secret spot #3 behind the STEM building.

TRISSA: Less super secret NOW hahaha. See you after school, Skull Girl :)

DREW: I don't know about that name.

TRISSA: What IS with all the skulls anyway?

DREW: I don't really know. I started doing it in grade school. They're just cool I guess.

TRISSA: Fair. Okay, well we can find you a shiny new nickname, if you want ;)

I realize as I read the text that I'm smiling. The truth is, I do kind of like Skull Girl, the more I think of it. When Trissa says it, it doesn't sound like she'd rather be around anyone but me. In fact, it almost sounds like she thinks I'm . . . cool because of it? I feel silly even thinking that, but it still makes me feel good. Like it's my code name.

Since we're watching a documentary, I review my notebook on the sly. Shrey, Trissa, and I decided to interview the two other victims after school—Connor Brady and Holly Reiss. Fortunately, they both go to Ella Baker's after-school program, so we can catch them at the same time. My eyes dart over the page as I look at my next victim profiles:

VICTIM PROFILE

NAME: Connor Xavier Brady
AGE: 12 **RACE:** Black
EYES: Brown **HAIR:** Bleached Blond
KNOWN HOBBIES: Music, theater, and musical theater
OFFENSE COMMITTED AGAINST VICTIM: A video was posted, seemingly taken in the Ella Baker multipurpose room, of Connor's voice cracking as he attempted a solo. The nickname of Squeakers was offered.

I don't know Connor well, being more into science and (murder) history than theater arts. I do, however, know that he came out as gay at the end of last year. For the most part, Connor got support. Some other kids said he was "brave," which I kind of hate because it's a word people only say when they don't get it.

Frowning, I move on to scan Holly's profile.

NAME: Holly Rae Reiss
AGE: 12 **RACE:** White
EYES: Brown **HAIR:** Dark Brown
KNOWN HOBBIES: Drawing (especially Disney-style hand animation), reading (especially graphic memoirs)
OFFENSE COMMITTED AGAINST VICTIM: Holly was featured in a video eating pizza rapidly. The post was a fat-shaming split image with Jabba the Hutt from Star Wars.

Even though Holly and I don't often cross paths, I feel like I understand her more since the post came out. I wasn't that overweight during the Fatface years, but I still remember the sting of shame from how kids talked to me. It wasn't just that I was fat; it was something else. I was an abnormal *shape*. Looking down at my pastry belly, I think, *I guess I still am.* And now, with everyone starting to look more grown-up (especially in the chest area) and being interested in kissing and all, my differences are even more obvious.

Well, this time, the bullies aren't going to get away with it, I think to myself. *With Connor and Holly, or with me. We're going to catch Ella Baker Shade if it kills me.*

10

"SO, YOU THREE ARE, like, school detectives?" Holly asks us. She grabs a small section of her hair, pulling one curl straight and regarding us nervously.

"Or cops?" Connor adds.

"Nothing like that," Trissa assures them.

"We're just trying to shut down Ella Baker Shade," I explain. My pen is poised to paper, my notebook open to the next blank page. "To do that, we need some information from both of you—" I break off, noticing a group of students eating their free after-school snack by the blue columns that line the cafeteria. We're a few feet away, but I still usher the group further toward the side of the building. When we're tucked away, right under a huge painted Ella Baker Badger mural, I go on. "So. Can you tell me how the posts have affected you?"

Connor snorts. "Well, I'm not wild about the whole Squeakers thing. Especially since I *know* Brian Wu must have seen it. Ugh. I've got the hugest crush on him. But, honestly? I've had worse, teasing-wise."

Shrey winces. "Yeah?"

"Well, yeah," Connor says. "Since I came out last year, Johnny Granday has made some dumb jokes. Alicia Alongie too. Mostly just laughing—but mean laughing, you know? And there's this one kinda racist kid, Micah."

Trissa immediately rolls her eyes. "Tell me about it. Last time I saw him in the library, he held up a book with a random Black girl on the cover and asked if it was me. It looked *nothing* like me. Then he asked if I was going to make Ms. Woodrich assign that book too."

"Too?" I repeat, confused.

She pauses, then explains, "I asked her to add more books by Black authors to our group reads. I guess Micah overheard."

Shrey rolls his eyes. "It would help if teachers actually *read* books by people who look like us, instead of assigning us the same white authors every year. I don't know if I've ever seen a book on our lists by an Indian author."

"And why do we always have to be the ones to bring this stuff up?" Connor points out.

"Right?" Trissa exclaims.

Connor, Trissa, and Shrey trade knowing looks.

I open my mouth to speak, but then quickly shut it. While I've definitely had a lot of pain in my life, I don't have experience with this. I know it happens, because my best friend has brown skin. And I live in Oakland. But there are still things I know I'll never really *understand*, because I'm white.

"What about you?" Shrey asks Holly, who seems to be trying her best to disappear into the background of the conversation. "Were you getting bullied a lot before the post?"

"Yes," she says in the smallest possible voice. Then she closes her eyes and clears her throat. "Yes," she repeats, louder this time. "I'm pretty quiet, but I cry really easily. My dad says crying can make kids meaner."

"True," I say, nodding with more understanding than she knows.

"I don't know why being shy is such a terrible thing. But they seem to just come after me. Micah Demmers points it out *every time* my face turns red. And Johnny. One time he said I was . . ." She trails off, cheeks reddening as if on cue.

"You can tell us," Trissa says. She puts an arm around Holly as tears spill down her face.

I shoot Trissa an admiring look. She isn't bad at this!

"Johnny started telling people that I had to go to the zoo doctor because I was a h-h-hippo." Holly lets out a little sob, but then sniffs and composes herself.

If it were possible for steam to be coming out of my ears right now, it would be. "That is *awful*," I say through clenched teeth. The words don't suffice, but I can't think of anything better.

Connor pulls Holly into a bear hug without hesitation. Trissa joins in, and even Shrey reaches out and puts a hand on Holly's arm. The whole thing makes me feel like an outsider—the girl who doesn't hug. I wonder if they think I'm this big emotionless robot for staying rooted to the spot.

"I'm really sorry, Holly," I say awkwardly, because I feel like I have to do *something*.

"See, this is why I think it has to be Johnny, Micah, or Alicia," Connor says after the hug breaks up and Holly looks at all of us gratefully. "Especially Johnny. He's a troll to, like, *everyone*."

"He's definitely a top suspect," I say, still distracted from my thoughts a moment ago. "What we're looking for is a pattern of behavior. Like how profilers catch criminals." Connor and Holly give me curious looks, but I can't seem to *stop*. "Because, you know, Johnny has a pattern of behavior just like thieves and murderers. Except I guess he doesn't kill people. Or maybe he does! You never know, right?"

OBSERVATIONS:

- Connor is staring at me with a gaping mouth.
- Shrey is leveling me with the exact same warning look he gave me at Eden Dodson's birthday party.
- Holly is still sniffling, but looks at me curiously.
- Trissa has cringe face.

CONCLUSION: I've made it weird. Yet again.

"I—I mean," I stutter, "we're absolutely looking at Johnny."

"Don't feel bad, Drew," Holly offers. "My dads are super into this true crime podcast called *Trackers*. It's these two retired detectives that solve cold cases. It's cool, but scary sometimes!" She shudders, but doesn't look at me like I've grown a second head.

"My sister listens to *Trackers*!" Connor says.

I let out a long breath, relieved to be let off the hook this time.

"Hey, Holly," Connor says, holding up his phone to show the time. "We've got to get back to the academy before they take away our Badger points for the day."

"Oh, yeah," Holly says, glancing at Connor and then back at us. "Good luck finding the Shade. And . . . thanks. For, you know, actually trying to."

"Seriously," Connor says. "Thanks for stepping up."

We all say our goodbyes, and Shrey doesn't waste any time before rounding on me. "Maybe Johnny Granday *kills* people?" He repeats my earlier words, laughing. "Drew, you are my best friend. But you have no filter."

"Filters are for suckers." Trissa shrugs.

I give her a thankful look. "So, everyone seems to suspect that Johnny is the culprit at this point, right? Ethan said the same thing—that he picks on everyone."

"You won't get any argument from me," Shrey says. "That guy is a grade-A jerk."

"True." I rub my chin thoughtfully. "I do question whether Johnny Granday has the skills for this. I mean, the last post had a hacked image from Mr. Clark's Facebook page. And there's the edited Holly video. He doesn't seem smart enough to have secret tech powers. Trissa giggles. "Are we talking about Granday's puny brain again?"

"Again?" Shrey raises an eyebrow.

"Skull Girl and I were texting about it during fourth. What do you think, Shrey? Is his brain more stone-fruit sized or are we talking sunflower seed? I'm guessing sunflower seed. Like, it's only good for 'Eat, sleep, punch.'" Trissa says the last few words Hulk-style, and I laugh.

"Sunflower seed," Shrey says slowly.

"Agreed," I say with a nod. "He doesn't seem capable of any brain power that could be called . . . advanced."

Trissa laughs, jabbing me playfully in the ribs. "You think?"

I rub my rib cage gingerly, but offer her a smile. This is a friend thing, right? Good-natured shoving? I see kids doing it on TV shows all the time, and *Dad* and I do it constantly. Why doesn't it feel natural with people my own age?

Remembering Holly and my inability to hug, I impulsively decide to return the gesture. I give her a playful shove back, and she falls over, giggling.

"Anyway. What do we do next?" Shrey cuts in. For

some reason, he looks annoyed. Is he mad that we're dismissing Johnny Granday as a suspect because Johnny bullied him? Or maybe he's mad that I texted Trissa instead of him about Ethan. I make a mental note to create a group thread for the three of us.

Trissa sits upright and pulls her legs in, crisscross-applesauce. "Okay, so I have this friend from Cesar Chavez who could help us with more information about Micah Demmers. Which we're looking for, right?"

"We are," I confirm. "Who's your friend? Do they know Micah from his old school?"

Trissa nods. "Yep, She goes to the International Charter School on Thirty-Fifth, where Micah went last year. Her name's Tiana—like the princess," Trissa says, then waves a finger as she adds, "Trissa and Tiana."

"Did you know her from Cesar Chavez?" Shrey asks.

"Yeah. Our moms have been friends since forever, *and* we were the only Black Jedi girls at Chavez. Into the whole fandom, that is."

"You guys pick a lightsaber color?" I ask with a knowing expression.

"Me, green; her, blue. It fits. Anyhow, she's coming over to my house Friday night to binge *Star Wars: Rebels*. It'll be the perfect time to ask her about Micah. She warned me about him when he showed up at Ella Baker this year. I'll bet she could give us a lot more about him leaving the International School. Maybe he was expelled or something?"

"That's *awesome*," I say. "So . . . should we meet back at the library tomorrow?"

"Oh, I almost forgot!" Trissa exclaims. "Comedy Club is in the library Thursdays, and I'm performing tomorrow. I can't meet up tomorrow at lunch. But I don't want to miss a day. It feels like we're really narrowing down our suspect list!"

I try not to give Trissa a sideways look, but, man, this girl is full of surprises. Comedy Club? Excited by the prospect of a narrowed suspect list?

"We won't miss a day," I promise. "Maybe it would be better if we met outside of school anyway. Dad's working late tomorrow. We could meet at my place."

"Fine by me!"

"Shrey, are you in?" I ask hopefully.

Shrey gives me a thumbs-up. "Yep, Dad won't be home until after dinner, and Mom's working a graveyard like usual. I was going to hang at your house anyways."

"A graveyard shift?" Trissa asks.

"My mom's an ER nurse."

"No way!" she says. "At Alta Bates? That's where my mom works. She's a NICU doctor."

"No, my mom's at Kaiser. She works really odd hours. I don't get to see her as much as I see my dad or my grandma."

I nod like I'm taking it in, but it isn't new information for me. Shrey ends up having a lot of dinners with my family—in spite of the fact that Bhavya is always saying that Shrey should "make a few new friends."

She's not the only adult who says I'm holding Shrey back from being a "normal" human being. When I was in the hospital with pneumonia, our fourth-grade teacher, Ms. Garcia, sat Shrey down and told him he should distance himself from me because I was "dragging him down socially." As if being bullied and having dumpster-fire lungs was *my* fault.

"Okay," I say, brushing off the memory. "Tomorrow after school, you both meet at my place at five-ish. Does that work?"

After everyone agrees, Trissa runs off to catch her bus, and Shrey and I start the steep walk uphill toward our houses.

"So." Shrey gives me the same unreadable look as he had earlier. "Trissa's pretty cool."

"She really is," I say, and then glance back toward school and ask, "Hey, don't you have baseball practice or whatever?"

"Drew. You were at my playoffs game two weeks ago. We didn't make the championship this year, remember?"

"Basketball?"

Shrey laughs. "We're between seasons."

"Wait, I knew that! Because the Warriors start in December, right? So basketball season starts in . . . January, right?" I jump up and down with glee as though I've solved a complicated puzzle.

"I need to find you some kind of book that blends sports facts with murder," Shrey says. "Then we could actually talk about the games."

"Karrie and Grace did one *Crime and Waffles* episode about O. J. Simpson," I reply hopefully.

"Well, at least you're trying."

I glance at Shrey to make sure he's not actually mad, and breathe with relief to see he's grinning. "Ha ha. Okay, so I might not be the biggest sports nerd. But I *do* know who Steph Curry is."

"Everyone knows who Steph Curry is."

"But does everyone know your epic skills of fart-bending?" I offer slyly.

He makes a loud noise that proves my point.

We both bust up laughing as we walk up the hill, and it occurs to me that today it really *does* feel like me and Shrey again. Texting about video games instead of feelings. No weird moments. No questions about me liking girls or the dreaded kissing subject.

At this moment, I've never been so happy to be talking about basketball and bodily functions.

11

DREW: Welcome to the FBI Special Agent Mega Crime-Solving Trio text thread!

DREW: Who has two thumbs, and just finished her last victim profile?

DREW: This girl!

TRIHSOKA TANO: I always believed in you.

DREW: Trissa. When you grabbed my phone yesterday, did you change your contact name?

TRIHSOKA TANO: Guilty! Gave myself a special ringtone too. Muhahahaaa, guess I'm more stealthy than you give me credit for!

SHREY: I have several issues with this text group name.

DREW: Ooh! You made the Star Wars Imperial March your ringtone!

TRIHSOKA TANO: You know it ;)

SHREY: Problem #1 FBI Special Agent? Really? You're the only one who's into that stuff.

DREW: Ugh, FINE. What would you prefer?

SHREY: Problem #2 Mega means LARGE. Three people isn't "mega" by any means. That is all.

SHREY: For a group name, I'd prefer something like "Jedi Detective Agency." We're all three of us Star Wars nerds and it sounds better.

DREW: First of all, two issues isn't several! MATH FAIL! Second, I'm into the Jedi Detective Agency. That'll work.

TRIHSOKA TANO: Seconded. I call Ahsoka, obvs.

DREW: I call Leia!

SHREY: Han Solo!

DREW: Eh, you're more of a Luke type.

SHREY: WHAT?

DREW: C3P0? Jar Jar?

SHREY: I hate you.

TRIHSOKA TANO: Do I need to leave this thread to let you two work out your issues? I'm in the library, waiting for my turn to improv btw so I'll have to pop out in a second.

TRIHSOKA TANO: Why are you even texting each other, aren't you eating lunch together? Y'all are weird.

SHREY: We are together. We just wanted to text you. Also, I only feel safe expressing my concerns about Drew's terrible group-naming skills in text form.

SHREY: Now she's trying to melt my face with her evil eye.

DREW: I WILL MELT YOU!

SHREY: Help, Trissa! Heeelllppppppp!

TRIHSOKA TANO: Nerds. Has your face melted yet, Shrey?

SHREY: Yes. It's everywhere.

DREW: The maintenance staff are coming to mop him up as we speak.

TRIHSOKA TANO: Are you two actually sitting on the blacktop texting each other? Mr. Lopez is gonna take your phones.

DREW: Oh, no. Didn't we tell you? We wanted to watch you improv. So, we went ahead and got seats in the back. Shrey, let's wave in 1 . . . 2 . . .

SHREY: 👋

***

SMS; Trihsoka Tano and Drew

TRIHSOKA TANO: I can't believe you and Shrey showed up. Also, I have to ask. Are you guys a couple?

DREW: A couple of BEST FRIENDS maybe.

TRIHSOKA TANO: You SURE?

DREW: 100%

TRIHSOKA TANO: Alright. But don't think I believe you. Maybe I need to solve my own mystery. The mystery of why you're hiding this romance. I HEARD what I HEARD.

DREW: Wait what?

TRIHSOKA TANO: About some kissing thing? Pretty sure I picked that up that very clearly.

DREW: You mean when you stalked us on Tuesday? That wasn't what it sounded like.

TRIHSOKA TANO: If you say so . . .

***

SMS; Drew and Shrey

SHREY: I did NOT see that coming. Trissa is FUNNY.

DREW: Right?!

SHREY: I mean, that one kid called out Yemen for a location and she just rolled with it. How does she know that much about Yemen?

DREW: How do ANY of us know about Yemen?

SHREY: What?

DREW: Oh. Nevermind. Sorry, I was distracted.

SHREY: By . . . ?

DREW: Micah Demmers walked by me in the hall and I wanted to see if I could read his expressions for possible guilt indicators.

SHREY: . . . because of course you were.

DREW: Ha ha. Anyway what were you saying about Yemen?

SHREY: Eh, nothing. Did you catch any guilt indicators or whatever?

DREW: Nah. He just looks like a jerk, like all jerks do.

SHREY: There has to be a word worse than jerks.

DREW: Well, there is, but I don't want to text it. My dad checks this phone. And I'm betting your dadi is receiving your texts by osmosis or something.

SHREY: No! My malai kofta!

DREW: Hey what about BUCKET?

SHREY: I'm sorry, were we talking about buckets?

DREW: No, I mean our made up bad word. Buckets sound all gross and filthy. Get away from me, ya bucket!

SHREY: I'll consider it.

SHREY: 🪣

DREW: Wait I don't have that. ARE YOU DOWN-LOADING EMOJIS WITHOUT ME?

SHREY: 🪣

DREW: I hate you.

12

"STOP LOOKING AT YOUR PHONE!" Dad explodes on the drive home.

I look up from texting Shrey a bucket-filled manifesto, because he won't stop taunting me with his new emoji.

"What? I'm not . . ." I trail off when I hear another text come in and glance back down at the screen.

"Oh, dear lord. Is this starting now?" Dad moans. "Am I going to need to become one of those dads that arranges screen-free nights for his kid? Follow-up question: can screen-free nights still have television?"

I roll my eyes, but the truth is he's really funny sometimes. "What were you saying?"

Dad moans theatrically. "I'm only trying to get the

details about this party and all these new friends. Because I love you. Even though you ignore me and break my heart."

"It's only *one* new friend, 'Dad.'" I say, making sarcastic air quotes with my fingers.

"Did you just air quote 'Dad' at me?"

"I felt it necessary, considering you're at risk of becoming one of '*those* dads' . . ." At this point I'm air quoting so hard that I'm at risk of spraining my fingers. "But it's not a party. We're probably going to watch TV or something."

"Okay. Well, if you want, I can come home early tonight and bring the pizza with me."

"No, don't cancel!"

The last thing I need is for Dad to catch me profiling with my new friends. Not because he wouldn't be proud, because he totally would. Mostly because he seems lighter these past few days. If he found out about all this Ella Baker Shade bullying stuff . . .

"You sure?" Dad asks as we pull into the driveway.

"Yeah."

Hopping out of the car, I wave at him from the driveway as he pulls away. I've barely kicked off my shoes before the doorbell rings.

At first, I assume it's Shrey. When he comes over for dinner during Bhavya's on-call shifts, he usually comes straight from school or practice. But it's Trissa in my doorway—holding what appears to be a zippered carpetbag and beaming at me.

"I'm going in!" she calls back toward a car in our driveway. Peering around Trissa, I see a smiling middle-aged woman waving.

"Have fun, Triss!" the woman calls brightly. She has close-cropped curly hair and Trissa energy.

"That's my mom," Trissa tells me, as though I hadn't already worked that out.

"Gotcha. Come on in!" I gesture toward the living room, where I've set up my crime board next to a stack of plastic cups and some soda. "Shrey should be here any minute."

Trissa immediately drops her oversized bag in the entryway and heads for the kitchen. It's not long before I hear a joyous shriek.

"Sorry!" she shouts. "Mama's on the Whole30 diet, and Dad only eats meat, so I'm, like, *obsessed* with other people's kitchens right now . . . WAIT, YOU HAVE SUGAR CEREAL?!"

"Only Choco-Crispers," I clarify. Though, now I'm

remembering that Dad's doing all the shopping. I guess there might be even more . . .

"And Sugar Bombs, and Jumble O' Honey, and . . ."

A brisk knock on the door interrupts this frenzied list, and I give Shrey an apologetic smile when I usher him in. "Trissa is very excited about our cereal selection," I explain over her shrieking.

"And Mo's O's and *Cake Flakes!*"

Yikes, is Dad eating his feelings right now?

"Okay, I was wrong; we have all the sugar cereals in the world. So, should I order pizza now, or . . . ?"

Trissa gives me an incredulous look. "Um, you do you. I'm eating *five* bowls of cereal, thank you very much."

After ordering a smaller pizza for the non-cereal-obsessed, I guide them to the living room, where I set up my crime board for viewing.

When Trissa sits down, she grabs our sixth-grade yearbook from the coffee table (I was scouring it the night before for clues). "This cover is so blah," she says, pointing at the generic Ella Baker Badger logo encircled by colorful figures holding hands. "My friend Liz's design was way better—she fully should have won that contest."

Shrey snags the book and looks down, reading, "Badgers in Unity? Meh."

I jump from foot to foot impatiently, and Shrey laughs.

"Let's see, what else can we talk about that isn't the case?" he says. "Torturing Drew is so easy . . ."

I make a loud harrumph, and he waves a hand toward me as if giving me permission to start.

"SO!" I begin, using my extendable pointer to reference the victim profiles in the center. "I've finalized every victim profile, including the ones for me and Trissa. I conclude that two likely perpetrators are emerging from this process."

"First!" I whip the pointer over to my suspects list. "We have Johnny Granday. Ethan Navarez is certain he's the culprit, and Connor and Trissa have also reported harassment. Johnny has targeted pretty much every victim, along with Shrey."

"It was mostly back at Cypress Grove," Shrey says to Trissa. "I've grown a lot since then."

"Can confirm," I say with a nod, using my pointer to poke Shrey in his chin.

"Hey, cut it out! Now you're bullying ME!"

"Nevertheless! We have several victims pointing the finger at Johnny Granday. But we also have quite a bit of evidence to support Alicia Alongie's guilt."

"Such as?" Trissa asks, rolling her hand expectantly.

"Such as the fact that I saw an incident report from August on Ms. Tuitasi's desk. It mentioned stealing passwords, and the incident took place during *second period*. Which is Alicia's technology period!"

"And mine, and Trissa's," Shrey points out. "Along with at least twenty other students. And how can you be sure it's even connected?"

"Also, I thought you said that Alicia didn't comment on any of the Ella Baker Shade posts," Trissa adds. "Wouldn't it fit your profile, or whatever, for her to be all over that?"

Tenting my hands, I regard them with barely contained glee. "Oh, that's what I thought, friends. Until I found *this!*" Theatrically, I whip the pointer toward a stapled set of papers pinned to the crime board. "I've been looking at the language in the comments section of the 'Badgers Ahoy!' posts by Ella Baker Shade. At first, I could only find the very obvious handles from our suspects: DemmersAttck, AliciAlongie and muyGranday. Obviously, Micah, Alicia, and Johnny. And a *super* obvious name from Alicia. A little too obvious? But then I studied the comments from a user named ShadyKT and compared it to my years of notes on Alicia's language patterns."

"Years of notes?" Trissa repeats, looking at Shrey.

"Don't ask," he tells her. He's shaking his head wildly as if to say, *Don't poke the bear!* but I ignore him and keep going.

"ShadyKT showed similar language patterns to Alicia *and* seemed to be egging the Shade on!"

"So?" Shrey asks.

"So . . . ShadyKT. As in Katie. Alicia's middle name being Katherine, and the troll's name also employing the word *shade* . . . I mean, I think we're all on the same trolley here, right?"

Shrey exchanges another look with Trissa, and then says, "It sounds good. But how do we prove it? The word *shade* isn't rare or anything. I think we need something solid to bring to Lopez if we want to turn this person in."

Deflated, I lower my pointer. "You're right," I confess. "This is barely even circumstantial evidence. But if we question our lead suspects, like Johnny—"

"Nope!" Shrey shouts. "Not in a million years!"

"Okay, then Trissa can come with me!"

"Trissa can do what, now?" Trissa yelps, whipping her head between Shrey and me. In spite of her faux fear, she mostly looks entertained.

"Okay, here's my thing," I say, dropping my pointer and grabbing my well-loved copy of *In the Shadow of a Killer*. "Lita says that the first steps to solving a crime are analyzing the scene and creating a timeline. We have no real way of doing either—not when the crime scene could be anyone's phone and it's easy to schedule posts. The next step is victimology, which we did. But now it's time to interrogate suspects." Letting out a long sigh, I clasp my hands together in a pleading gesture. "C'mon."

"C'mon?" Shrey scoffs. "Is that the best you've got?"

I roll my eyes. "No. The 'best I've got' is everything I said *before* that, ya bucket!!"

Shrey fixes me with a hard stare, and then brings his hands together for a reluctant and slow clap. "Well used. Don't you wish you had an *emoji* for that?"

"Okay," Trissa says, blinking rapidly. "I have no idea why you two are rambling about buckets, but I think Drew's right. Why don't we at least make a plan on how we could approach each suspect. Deal?"

Shrey and I maintain our staring contest until neither of us can take it anymore and we break down laughing.

"Okay," I say, still feeling light and giddy from my presentation. "Let's work on that after pizza."

"And more cereal!" Trissa shouts.

Predictably, all of us are too wired to get back on task after dinner. We end up doing the following, very-*not*-nerdy things to pass the time:

1) Taking a "Which Disney Princess Are You?" quiz for each of us. Survey says: I'm Mulan, Trissa is Rapunzel, and Shrey is . . . wait for it . . . Vanellope von Schweetz!

2) Watching the Ember Island Players episode of *Avatar: The Last Airbender* two times back-to-back while Shrey gushes about the glory of Sokka and his love of meat.

3) Busting out our family karaoke machine and using the microphone to sing this old Bill Murray version of the Star Wars theme my dad's obsessed with.

This, of course, is the moment Dad comes home . . .

"Staaaaaarrr Wars!" Trissa and I are singing a duet into the microphone while Shrey laughs maniacally. "Those near and FAR wars! Nothing but STAR WARS! Don't let them end . . ."

"What. Hath. I. Wrought?" Dad says as we sing the last few bars.

Trissa jumps down from the fireplace platform and envelops my dad in a hug. "Hi, Mr. Leclair! I'm Trissa, nice to meet you!"

Still wearing a look of sheer wonderment, Dad glances between all three of us. Then he turns to Trissa and says, "It is *very* nice to meet you, Trissa. Very nice."

"Sorry we made such a mess," I say, glad I had the

foresight to put the crime board back under my bed before we devolved into our dorky activities.

"Don't worry about that, sweetie. I just never thought I'd find you singing that song again—out of footie pajamas, at least. Why don't the three of you hang out in Drew's room while I clean up? Shrey, your dad called, and I have to drive you home in a few minutes."

"I'll call my mom!" Trissa announces as she follows Shrey down the hallway.

"Hey." Dad pulls me aside and whispers, "I love seeing you have fun." He pulls me in to kiss my head, but I wriggle away and playfully slug his arm.

I don't know why, but this is the moment I realize that I've gone the whole day without making an observation in my notebook. I can't remember the last time that happened. It's also the first day I haven't thought about Mom. Maybe I've thought about Ella Baker Shade and Dad finding out, but not Mom herself. I trail down the hall after my friends with a grin on my face.

When I walk into my room, I'm still smiling, but I get right to business: "Okay, we only have a few minutes. Let's start to brainstorm ways we can question—"

The melodic *bling!* of an Instagram notification interrupts me, and I scramble for my phone.

Trissa's eyes pop. "Who's that? I see the look on your face. You got a boooyyyfriend? Or giiirrrrlfriend?"

Shrey and I both redden. We find anything to look at in my room that isn't each other.

"No!" is my super unconvincing reply, even though it's true. "Nothing like that. I set a 'favorite people' notification for posts from Ella Baker Shade. I mean, ironically, since they might be one of my *least* favorite people . . . Wait."

"What?" Shrey asks.

Eyes wide, I hold my phone up.

Which Ella Baker student ripped her jeans after PE yesterday? Check out this fresh pic of the XXL underwear of our very own mean girl: Alicia Alongie!

13

"CAN WE WATCH IT AGAIN?" a sixth-grader I don't know is whispering to her friend. Like clockwork, I hear the cartoonish *rip!* of Alicia's jeans, along with a *super* fake farting noise.

"Bwahahahaha!" they screech on the other side of the library stacks. They're in the 700s, because of course they are. It's where all the cool kids hang out.

Pulling my knees to my chest, I wait alone in the good old 800s until Shrey and Trissa arrive. We'd talked about the post for a few minutes last night, but both of them had to go home, so we agreed to meet here for lunch. However, with Mr. Covacha's lax rules about cell phones, the library is now flooded with giggling students. I'm not sure it's the best place to talk. Maybe the garden would be quieter . . .

Rrrrrrrrrip, pppppfffffftttttthhh!

"Hahahaaaaa!"

Here we go again.

Look, I'll admit it. When I saw the post last night, I sort of thought Alicia deserved it. But it's a different story today. Seeing how people are treating Alicia makes me feel like I'm in a whole *school* of bullies. I know what a terrible person Alicia is. But the kids at school aren't just calling her *mean* (which she is); they're calling her fat. Which is a problem on more than one level. First, kids are treating fat like it's an insult instead of a body shape. Second, even though this post is about Alicia, *every* fat kid on campus feels bad.

I'd exchanged a long, sad look with Holly earlier as she shuffled across campus with her head down. Probably because, today, *everyone* in school is taking part in the shame game. Including people I thought were nicer.

"Heeyyyyy." Shrey says with wide eyes, chucking his backpack next to mine.

I look up and see Trissa trailing a little ways behind. "Hi." She greets us, following suit. The three of us huddle together next to our mini-mountain of backpacks, trying to stay quiet.

"So, obviously, Alicia's not here today," Trissa says.

"And she's probably off our suspect list," Shrey adds.

They look hopeful, as if asking my permission to cancel suspect questioning for today, but I refuse to lose our momentum. "You're right," I say. "But it's still time to talk to Micah and Johnny. There's *no* way Emma and Brie would cross Alicia like this. That's three suspects tentatively off our list."

"That makes things easier," Trissa says. She slugs Shrey. "Come on, Malhotra. If Drew can talk to Granday, we can too. Right?"

"I guess."

"That's the spirit!" I cheer. A buzz sounds from my phone, and I look down at it, even though I know what I'll see. "Ugh," I say. "More comments on the Alicia post. This is getting worse by the hour."

Shrey and Trissa exchange a look.

"Well, didn't she kind of ask for it?" Trissa points out carefully. "I mean, she's nasty. We all know it."

"She doesn't get any sympathy from me," Shrey agrees.

"Yeah, but people aren't attacking her for being nasty. They're saying things that could hurt everyone who looks like her!" Suddenly aware that heads are turning in my direction, I lower my voice and lean in closer.

"I can't believe you of all people are defending Alicia," Shrey says. "You have to admit it's kind of weird."

Looking between them, I hiss, "How can you not get this? It isn't about Alicia. It's about people like Holly, who will hear her friends laugh about Alicia being called fat and wonder what they really think about *her*."

Shrey looks thoughtful, but Trissa immediately flushes sheepishly.

"You're right," she says. "We're sorry. What can we do?"

"Thanks," I say. "Of course, the first thing we have to do is look at this change in victimization."

"Of *course*," Shrey says with an annoying sarcastic tone.

"I'm sorry, do I detect *snark* in your voice right now?"

He stiffens, backpedaling. "No ma'am."

"Is victimization like victimology?" Trissa asks, looking between us.

"Yes!" I say. "It's the selection of victims, like who someone decides to hurt or steal from. Lita says that the best way to understand a perpetrator is to understand the people they hurt. The Junipero Valley Killer, for example. He always had a certain type of victim. Ella Baker Shade changed victim type overnight, which almost *never* happens in a criminal investigation."

"But . . ." Trissa says slowly, "this isn't a criminal investigation."

"No, but this is a mystery that needs solving," I point out. "I think we need to talk to our suspects *now*. Starting with Johnny. It's time to see who we're dealing with."

***

QUESTIONS FOR JOHNNY GRANDAY (A.K.A. OUR #1 SUSPECT!)

1) What do you know about Ella Baker Shade?

2) Do you have any other accounts on Instagram other than "muyGranday"?

3) What is your history with the victims of these posts?

4) What's your favorite sport?

5) How do you like your pizza?

6) How did you come up with the name Ella Baker Shade?

This last one is from an the FBI interrogation technique I read about. It's where you ask a bunch of easy questions quickly, and then one important question to trick a perpetrator into confessing. I figure it's worth a shot.

I look down at the prompts in my notebook, mentally preparing as we walk up to Johnny and his crew. He's sitting with a group of boys up against the back gate, where he usually eats lunch on warm days.

It's almost as if, the minute we start toward Johnny, his group erupts into laughter. For a moment, the three of us trade a look as if to say, *Are we really doing this?* My feet feel like they're made of lead as I usher us toward the boys.

"Johnny," I say in my best professional voice. "Can we talk to you for a moment?"

Trissa and Shrey both give me openmouthed looks, and I wonder if they think I'm being too direct. Maybe they're right. Especially since the other boys with Johnny look just as mean.

Johnny rubs a hand through his gelled-slick brown hair. "Uhhhhh, why?"

I decide to go with a more stealthy approach to draw him away from the group. Earlier this year, I'd been looking for books in the library on Alcatraz (for more information on axe-wielding ghosts, obviously), and I saw Johnny's name in *all three* of the books our library has on the subject. Without anything better to go on, I state, "We're starting a petition to make Alcatraz our school trip, and we're interviewing students at random to find out who's interested."

Johnny raises an eyebrow. "Alcatraz? That would be cool. Didn't expect a good idea from *you*, Leclair. Or Malhotra over here."

Shrey gives him a weak smile as I drawl, "Thaaaaaanks?"

Johnny stands, telling his friends he'll be right back, and follows us a few feet down the breezeway. Even though we're only about ten feet away, we're that much closer to the library. It feels like our territory.

"So, are we gonna go inside the jail cells and everything?" Johnny asks, rubbing his hands together.

"Of course!" I say, wide-eyed. "The cells will be open, and we'll have the highest level tour. Where they tell us all the *really* bad stuff that happened there."

"Niiiice." He gives Trissa a wicked smile, and adds, "D'you think we'll see some *eye*balls?"

Trissa presses her mouth together in a tight, humoring smile. I can tell she's annoyed, though, since she keeps clicking her pen up and down with her thumb with enough force to cause her skin to flush.

Staring down at my notebook, I realize that I have

literally nothing about Alcatraz and everything on Ella Baker Shade. I could mention the ghost, but Johnny would just get into a Drew-Leclair-is-a-freak loop, and we don't have that kind of time. I decide to redirect the conversation right away. "Anyhow . . ." I begin, before Shrey clumsily breaks in.

"So, um, how about that, uh, Ella Baker Shade post today?"

I wince. Shrey's question is a few beats too quick, but Johnny doesn't seem to notice.

Letting out a sharp laugh, he says: "Yeah, that was sweet. I wish I could see the look on chubbo's face. Guess she's hiding at home today, huh?"

"Guess so," I say noncommittally.

"So, who do *you* think the Shade is?" Trissa asks.

Johnny rubs his jaw. "Oh. Uh, I dunno. Seems kind of like something you would do, Leclair. Everyone's always saying you're, like, some kind of stalker."

"It's not me," I reply, ignoring the jab. "I was in one of the posts, remember?"

Johnny laughs loudly and makes a kissy face. "Oh I *know*."

"Uh. Huh." I state flatly.

"Look, who knows who the Shade is?" Johnny says after he's done laughing at me. He tosses an appraising look at Shrey. "A few years ago I would have said Malhotra here would be small enough to hide around campus and get those videos. But I guess you grew. My boy's grown!" He grabs Shrey into an awkward half hug and shakes him.

Shrey reddens, and I can't tell if he's embarrassed or terrified. Why would Johnny think it was okay to hug him? Still, I take the uncomfortable moment to make a few notes:

OBSERVATIONS:

- Johnny has a ratty old Samsung cell phone hanging out of his pocket. Not exactly the model a tech person would have.
- Johnny isn't reacting noticeably when Ella Baker Shade is mentioned.
- Johnny speaks in very basic language, unlike our school cybertroll. That hasn't changed since grade school.
- He's hugging Shrey. SHREY.

CONCLUSION: Johnny may be our top suspect, but he doesn't add up as Ella Baker Shade.

"All right," I say as Johnny finally unhands a trembling Shrey. "Well, if you'll just give us your statement in support of the Alcatraz trip, we'll let you go back to lunch."

He gives me a nonsensical statement about how much he loves cops and guns, which I pretend to write down in my notebook. When Johnny sits back down with his friends, out of earshot, I turn to Shrey and Trissa.

"Well, that was awful," Shrey says, rubbing his shoulder.

"Yeah, I did not predict him *hugging* you," I say. "Sorry, buddy."

"That was hella weird," Trissa says.

"So here's the thing," I say in a hushed voice. "I don't like Johnny Granday."

Trissa snorts. "I don't like him either!"

Shaking my head, I say, "No, not like that. I mean the way detectives say they 'like' a suspect for a crime. I really don't think he makes sense as the Shade."

"What are you saying?" Shrey asks. "That Granday couldn't have done it?"

"Not necessarily," I say. "But does he seem like the type to hold on to embarrassing videos, or to be inconspicuous enough to get them in the first place?"

"Not really," Shrey agrees.

"I mean, after today, I even wonder if *he* knows how terrible he is," I suggest.

"He does seem to think everything is one big gag," Trissa agrees. "Like his whole eyeball remark? As if he's going to get me to barf again?"

"Exactly," I say. "I mean, I guess he could have an accomplice."

"Like Micah Demmers?" Trissa suggests. "Remember, I'm talking to Tiana tonight and can get more intel. Micah could definitely be working with Johnny."

"That's great," I reply. "We can wait until Monday to question him. But I've never seen the two of them together. And he's not any more stealthy than Johnny. Micah might be the perpetrator, but there isn't any evidence to support him as an accomplice."

"So, like Johnny said. We're looking for someone more like you," Shrey blurts. He immediately puts up his hands and waves them frantically. "I mean . . . I didn't mean . . ."

"No," I say, putting a finger to my chin thoughtfully. "You're right. You were right that first day, when I showed you the profile. We may not be looking for your garden-variety bully. We may be looking for someone *exactly* like me. A fellow victim."

14

"SO, YOU REALLY THINK we could be looking at one of the victims?" Shrey asks me as we walk off campus at the end of the day.

"Well, not victims of Ella Baker Shade," I clarify. "They wouldn't post something that embarrassing about themselves. Just a regular victim of bullying, or someone really quiet, I guess. I haven't really thought it through yet. There's that second period technology connection we could look into. Ella Baker Shade isn't Alicia, but maybe it's someone from that class?"

"Are you going to profile *me* next?" Shrey jokes.

"No, but our suspect list just got a lot longer. We do need to look into every lead. Can you get me a class list or something?"

"Sure thing," he says, scrolling with one finger on his

phone screen. "I actually have a class list in my email because Ms. Tuitasi sent us our group assignments. There. I just sent you a screenshot."

A little *bloop!* sounds, and I offer him a weak smile. "Thanks."

I don't say it aloud, but this whole day has drained me to the point where I wish I could walk home alone. Not that I'm mad at Shrey or anything. Just to clear my head.

I can't stop thinking about these bullies and what makes them tick. Usually, it's easy for me to put a finger on—especially with people like Alicia and Johnny. But this is different. The identity of Ella Baker Shade seems even further away from me now.

"Maybe we should look at people who haven't been in school lately," Shrey rattles on. "Like, could someone have been bullied so badly they left school and started doing this out of revenge?"

"Revenge on Alicia, maybe. But what about the others? It doesn't fit," I mutter. The idea of being bullied badly enough that you have to leave school is something I can relate to. Maybe Shrey is right about Ella Baker Shade being like me.

Scanning my memory, I try to remember a moment when I could have gone to the dark side after bullying.

After the *Ripley's Believe It or Not* incident, I remember joking with Shrey about filling Alicia's shoes with mud. But we hadn't gone through with it. How bad would the bullying need to be for a person to transform into someone as mean as Ella Baker Shade?

As I'm remembering that day, Mom flashes in my mind. She'd been the one to pick me up after Alicia, Brie, and Emma chased me with the grotesque bee-sting images. The memory is so vivid that I can almost smell Mom's Clinique perfume and see her fiery expression as she tells me, *You just say the word, kid. Say the word, and I'll make a stink like you've never seen, and I'll get those kids kicked out of school!*

She was so mad and protective of me that day. It's probably the best memory I have of her, but today it makes me think. Could Ella Baker Shade be a friend of someone who's been hurt? Could it be someone so upset that they lashed out, like Mom had threatened to do? But if that were true, why would they go after nice kids first, before Alicia?

No. It doesn't make sense. *None* of this makes sense.

And why couldn't Mom be that protective all the time? Why didn't she protect me from all the hurt *she'd* caused me?

Between my frustration and the invasive memory, the worst happens: the tears I've been holding at bay start spilling out, one after another. Sucking in a long breath, I manage to squeeze my eyes and stop them.

But not before Shrey sees my face.

"Hey, wait up . . . whoa," he says. "Stop, Drew. What's wrong?"

Ignoring him, I keep plodding up the hill.

"Wait!" Shrey catches up with me quickly—because of *course* the athletic kid catches up with the short-legged asthma kid—and blocks the sidewalk. "Stop."

I stop short and scan the area to make sure we're alone. When I see a group of Ella Baker students heading toward us, I pull Shrey into a driveway with foliage heavy enough to block us from view. "Look," I snap, "I'm fine, all right?"

"No you're not," Shrey says. "You're crying. Well, you were a second ago, at least. You never cry. In fact, I don't think I've seen you cry since fifth—"

"Why are you friends with me?" I blurt. Humiliatingly, the question comes out like a thick, snotty whine.

Shrey laughs, which makes me want to cry all over again, but I don't.

"I'm serious!"

"C'mon! You know why. You're awesome. You're more fun than anyone else our age. You don't make fun of me for the nerd stuff — like, for example, you're the only one at school I could have texted about the Super Paper Mario sequel. Nobody else knows about that game."

"That's true," I sniff. "But only because it came out, like, when we were born."

"You come to more of my games than my parents do," Shrey goes on, "even if I know you're secretly reading your true crime stuff the whole time. Why? Because I ask you to. I mean, you're a pain in the butt sometimes, but you're also really loyal like that."

"Why wouldn't I go to your sports games?"

Shrey laughs. "For one, because you call them 'sports games.' You're clearly not interested, but you do it anyway."

Sniffing, I say, "I do."

"Also, you're funny — maybe the funniest person I've ever met. Ever since that day in first grade, I knew you'd be my best friend."

"The day with the Fruity Nuggets?"

"Yeah. Who else would put a mouthful of dry cereal in her mouth and say, 'Look at me! I'm a *cereal* killer'?"

"And who else would get that joke?" I retort.

"Drew. I was six. I had no idea what you were talking

about. I went home and asked my mom what a 'cereal killer' was, and she freaked out and told me never to sit with you again."

"Fair," I say with a laugh.

"Why are you asking me all of this?" Shrey gives me a quizzical look, and I realize how out-of-the-blue this must seem to him.

"I'm just thinking about all the kids who never found a Shrey."

"What?"

"Look, you've been my only friend . . ." I begin.

"And you're my only friend," he counters.

"But not really, though," I say. "Maybe I'm your only best friend, but you hang out with other people. You know—those guys in your sports games."

"Sure, we hang out after games. But they're not my real friends. You are, because I get to be *full Shrey* with you. As in, wizard robes, special-edition lightsaber, Appa plush, my weird obsession with cave documentaries—Shrey . . . the whole me. But, Trissa is our friend too now. Right?"

"Yeah, it looks like she might be. It's not that," I insist. "I was only thinking . . ."

"About kids who never found a magnificent Shreyas Malhotra?" He strikes a heroic pose.

I crack up, almost pausing to make a joke about the "glory that is Shrey," when something holds me back.

OBSERVATIONS:

- We're standing alone in a random vine-lined driveway, completely hidden from view.
- Shrey is looking (or possibly *gazing*) at me right now.
- There is only, like, six inches between us.

CONCLUSION: Warning! Possible kissing opportunity!

I *can't* let him kiss me again. If he kisses me, I'll hate it, and I'll have to explain *why* I hate it. And I'm not ready to answer any of the questions he has about who I am, or who I like, or why I'm not interested in kissing anyone.

"Hey. Drew?" Shrey says in a low voice. He doesn't move closer, but shifts uncomfortably, looking nervous. "There's something I need to ask you. I—"

"Whoa!" I interject, giving him a light punch on the

arm. "Look at the time! Good talk, but I've got to get home before my dad comes back from the bakery."

Shrey looks doubtful, to say the least. "You mean to your house that's a half mile away before your dad gets home in three *hours*?"

"Ummm, yes? Look, he's probably going to call home. I've got to be there. See you tomorrow, 'kay?" The last few words come out in a clumsy tangle as I trip backing away from him. I'm very graceful. "Bye!"

Shrey's hurt and bewildered face is the last thing I see before I turn on my heel and stride away, tears stinging my eyes.

Why am I so terrible at being a person?

Just when I think my day can't get any worse, my phone rings, the contact screen flashing with literally the *last* person I want to talk to. As in: I'd prefer a group Facetime call with Alicia Alongie, Johnny Granday, *and* the Junipero Valley Killer. The word, large and blaring on the screen, reads MOM.

Ugh.

I reject the call, obviously. But I can't stop myself from listening to the voicemail:

"Hi, Drew, it's your mom. Just calling to see if we can talk about this. I really miss you, sweetheart. I wish you would let me explain. You know, family is a two-way street.

I've called you twice now. I think you're being really imma-tur—oh, wait. Okay need to get this call. Bye, sweetie!"

Well, I guess every garbage sundae needs a cherry on top. And, after the day I've had, that message is the perfect topper. She can't even leave a voicemail without: 1) totally ignoring my feelings and 2) blaming *me* for our lack of communication. Even though the message enrages me, I feel a stab of guilt at ignoring her call when I know how much Dad wants me to talk to her.

I delete the voicemail and shove my phone in my pocket, imagining that erasing the message actually erases her. Grimacing, I pick up my pace until our little green house comes into view. When I get inside, I head right for the shower, figuring that scalding water can wash this awful day down the drain.

I end up spending the duration of my shower repeating the mantra: *Don't cry. You're a scientist. No emotion!* As I towel dry my hair, I start to wonder: is my emotion problem basically the same as Elsa from *Frozen*, but without the magical powers?

When I dry off and return to my room, I immediately reach for my old standby—*In the Shadow of a Killer.* Who knows? Maybe Lita has advice on what to do when:

1) Your entire investigation changes direction.
2) Your school becomes a den of jerks.

3) Your mom loves yurts more than she loves you.
4) Your best friend is sure you're gay because you won't kiss him, but you don't even know what you are.

Seeing as how 2 through 4 are pretty personal, I scan to see if she has thoughts on the first point. "Aha!" I say, as I find a passage titled "When All Leads Run Cold":

> When you hit a dead end with a suspect, the depres-
> sion is not unlike a broken heart. We like a suspect
> until an alibi or evidence proves us wrong. When
> this came up during the Junipero Valley Killer case,
> I had to take some time to mourn the loss of that
> cold lead.

Oh, Lita! Is there anyone else who could possibly understand my agony right now? Especially since I have a shiny new problem: my suspect list is much longer now. Before the Alicia post, Ella Baker's serial-offender bullies seemed to be the only option. Now, with the idea that the Shade could be a victim, I could be looking at half the school.

After an hour of brainstorming on the crime board, I give up and head to my dresser to jammy up. After rummaging around for a minute, I settle on a loose tee featuring Eleven from *Stranger Things* (eating Eggos, be-

cause of course she is), and my matching Hawkins A.V.
Club sweats.

Eleven. She's a fictional girl that I sort of crush on.
But less in a for-sure-gay way and more in an I-want-
telekinetic-powers-in-my-life way. Still. That ticks one
more box for Shrey's theory that my lack of interest
means something.

I'm just starting to drift off, imagining Eleven de-
molishing Ella Baker Shade with her powers, when I
hear the front door creak open.

Wait, is Dad home? Why is he this early?

Swiftly, I shut my laptop and kick the edge of the
crime board under my bed to make sure it's hidden.

"Dad?"

No one answers.

Dad *always* calls out when he gets home. The dead
noise, followed by shuffling footsteps, gets me from zero
to freaked out in seconds. *Is* that Dad? Could it be someone else? A *murderer* perhaps?

The heavy plodding sound of footsteps moves down
the hall . . . and stops right in front of my room.

15

MY MIND SWIRLS WITH POSSIBILITIES. Maybe Lita was wrong about the Junipero Valley Killer, and he (or *she*) is here to get me!

Nope. Lita is never wrong.

Could it be Ella Baker Shade? Our address is listed in the school directory, which goes home with every kid.

Wait. It could be *Mom*. Maybe she's coming home early from Kauai because Dustin fell into a volcano. The thought of Mr. Clark getting chucked into hot lava makes me smile for a second. As I stand frozen at my door, I wonder: who would I rather be faced with right now? A murderer, a bully . . . or my mom?

The floor creaks under the weight of whoever is standing by my door, and I realize the obvious answer: a murderer is worse. *Way* worse.

I'm frozen in place on the bed, absolutely sure that the doorknob is going to start twisting in that super-creepy "the killer is coming inside!" way. My heart hammering in my chest, I stare at the doorknob. My stinging eyes finally manage to blink when the footsteps resume, plodding further down the hall.

"Dad?" I yell again, louder this time.

"Uhhhh-um. Yeah. I'll be right there, okay?" Dad calls back in a strained voice.

My stomach is a roller coaster, rapidly spinning me from fear to relief to worry. Why does Dad sound weird? Instead of waiting, I creep down the hallway and peer through his cracked door.

"Dad?" I ask again, more tentatively.

He doesn't seem to hear me, so I push the door open.

When I see him, I stop in my tracks. He's crying again, but it's the *way* he's crying. It's not a few stray tears, or wiping at wet eyes. He's sobbing. Uncontrollably.

It reminds me of when I was little and didn't want to go to bed. He's crying in a way I didn't know grownups *could* cry.

A sting at the corners of my eyes tells me I might be in danger of crying too. But I don't.

If I cry, he'll just cry harder, and it'll be my fault. Instead, I move toward his hunched form on the bed and rest a hand on his back. He jerks up fast enough that I jump. Then he crumples back into his bent-over position. I know I should be strong right now, but the way he's crying scares me to the point where I feel like I'm standing on a ledge without a rope or an anchor. Like my person — the one who's supposed to pull me back—is gone.

"I'm sorry, sweetie," he chokes out. "You don't need to see me this way. I'll be right out, okay?"

Part of me is so freaked out by this that I want to do what he says. But I can't leave him. I sit down and wrap my arms around him tightly—like he used to do when I would get the medicine-induced shakes.

Dr. Miyamoto says that sometimes running out of options can lead you to the answer you're seeking. Maybe it's like that with hugs. The energy that's trying to get out has no choice but to settle when your body is squeezed too tight to move.

I can tell Dad's resisting me, but he finally leans in, and his sobs quiet after a while.

"I'm okay," he says.

"Is it . . . Is it Mom?"

"In a way." His voice is low as he adds, "I just don't know how to be this new person."

"Why can't you be *you*?"

"I don't mean your dad." He gives me a squeeze. "I

always know how to be your dad. I don't know how to be . . . a guy without a wife."

"I get that," I say, even though I don't at all. I spot something barely peeking out from Dad's messenger bag. Squinting, my eyes widen when I see what it is: the PTO flyer.

"Um, did something happen at the PTO meeting?"

Dad looks as if he's holding back from saying something, but says, "No. Nothing like that. I'm being over-sensitive. I promise, okay?"

"Are you sure? I mean, you were just there, and now you're upset."

"Yes, I'm sure. It wasn't the meeting." He grabs the flyer, along with another printed sheet. "I even grabbed an agenda for next time. Look, you just worry about normal kid stuff. Like your new friends, okay? I love that you're spending so much time with them these days."

He smiles warmly, but I can't help obsessing on the question: *Am I spending TOO much time with them and not with Dad?*

I'm terrified of saying the wrong thing, so I say the only thing I can think of. "Um, do you want to watch *Trail of Blood*?"

I'm afraid I've crossed a line when I hear a small high-pitched noise coming from Dad.

He's laughing.

"Hey, Bun. You know I love you more than anything, right?" Dad says when his laughter dies down. He hasn't called me Bun since I was six, but I don't feel embarrassed or annoyed. It makes me feel safe.

"I love you, too," I say. "So is that a yes to *Trail of Blood*? I can order a pizza in under thirty minutes."

He gives me a sly smile. Sometimes I do say the right thing.

"Yes," he says. "Go order the pizza and give me five minutes, okay? I'm going to take a shower."

I nod, watching as he disappears into the attached bathroom. It's not long before my eyes wander back down to the PTO flyer. Peering at the now-closed bathroom door, I grab the flyer and agenda and scan the words. My stomach drops when I read

Agenda items for special 10/29 meeting:
  1) Cyberbully issue at EBMS

That's just next week! And if they're talking about Ella Baker Shade, then Mr. Lopez is almost surely running the special meeting. I've observed at least three PTO meetings in the library after school. So far as I've seen, the vice principal only shows up if there's a major disciplinary issue to talk about. If he's there next week, he could tell Dad about the posts.

And the message I deleted.

Retrieving my phone from my pocket, I rush back toward my room. How did I get wrapped up in the Ella Baker Shade case to the point where I forgot my original objective: *to protect DAD?*

Was everyone talking about the posts at the meeting? They must have been, if it's on a special agenda for next week. If they were talking about the posts, they were probably gossiping about Mom and Mr. Clark too. It must have been awful for him, with everyone whispering. And I was too busy having fun with my friends to even notice.

Squeezing my eyes shut, I take out my notebook. I can't wait for a whole weekend to work on the case. The meeting is the night of Fall Fest—right before break. I have to move forward on my own.

There's also the fact that, after today, it seems like anybody could be a suspect. Which means I'm already running out of time. My eyes fall toward the open book on my desk. What was it that Lita said about perpetrators? It was the same thing I remembered when Trissa approached us this week. *A criminal can insert themselves into an investigation by offering to help.* Could Ella Baker Shade be closer than I think?

My stomach turning, I check my phone and scan the class list that Shrey sent me. Alicia Alongie, Holly Reiss, Shreyas Malhotra, Faizah Abad, Samantha Vazquez, Trissa Jacobs . . .

Both Shrey and Trissa are in that second period class from the incident report. And both of them have been the victim of bullying. Which potentially hits two points in my emerging profile. A lump forms in my throat that doesn't disappear even when I swallow.

My friends could be suspects.

"Hey, honey!" Dad's tired voice calls out. "Did you order the pizza yet?"

I scramble to make a quick order on my phone and then call back, "Yeah! Delivery in thirty!"

It couldn't be Shrey and Trissa. Right? But Lita always says to follow every lead. Shouldn't I write out a profile, just to eliminate them as suspects? Maybe I should just do it fast, so I can focus on starting the rest. Hands shaking, I scribble out two new profiles:

SUSPECT PROFILE

NAME: Shreyas Hardik Malhotra
AGE: 12 **RACE:** South Asian

EYES: Brown **HAIR:** Black

KNOWN HOBBIES: Collecting Funko Pops, sportsball, coding (but mostly in Super Mario Maker to create new levels), possible new interest in romance?

POSSIBLE MOTIVE: Shrey has always been mad about people like Johnny Granday avoiding punishment. Could he be posting as Ella Baker Shade to point the finger at him somehow? Shrey was also mad at Drew for not kissing him back. Could this have caused him to turn on Drew?

COUNTERPOINT: Drew's best friend, and usually nice. Would he do this?

***

SUSPECT PROFILE

NAME: Patricia "Trissa" Jacobs
AGE: 12 **RACE:** Black
EYES: Brown **HAIR:** Black
KNOWN HOBBIES: Fashion, improv comedy,

Star Wars, reading, pin trading
(assumed, based on the massive number
of Disney pins on her backpack that
are recognized from Pin Traders at
Disneyland).

POSSIBLE MOTIVE: Trissa seems nice (as
evidenced by membership in Random Acts
of Kindness Club) and from all recent
observations (i.e., being a good friend),
but could this be a lie? Suspect might
be pretending to forge a bond with the
profiler in order to deflect guilt from
herself. More evidence is needed in order
to prove guilt.

COUNTERPOINT: It is unlikely that Trissa
would post about herself.

I set my pen down after I finish and look at my work.
Even though everything I said is true, writing the words
leads to a stab of regret that comes in the form of a gur-
gling stomach cramp.

*Come on, Leclair. You're just being practical and look-
ing at every piece of evidence.*

*Didn't you read a Nancy Drew book where Nancy sus-
pects her boyfriend, Ned Nickerson, of sabotage? She didn't*

eliminate him based on a feeling. Could NANCY DREW be wrong?

It's not like I'm not going to profile everyone else, too. I have to if I'm going to find Ella Baker Shade by next week. How could they get mad if I'm looking at everyone that fits the profile?

The justifications buzz in my mind, but they aren't enough to take the guilt away. I tear both pages out of the notebook and consider ripping them up for a half second. But I can't.

Every lead, I remind myself. I hastily fold up the profiles and shove them under an Obi-Wan Kenobi Mickey plush on my desk. Immediately, I feel my tension lift.

Out of sight, out of mind.

16

"AARRLLGGG. I WANT TO COMPOSE an epic haiku about this croissant," Trissa tells me as we sit on the plush velvet bar stools of Leclair's Eclairs.

"Haikus are literally the opposite of epic," I point out. "Do you need to be alone with your pastry?"

"Maybe," she says.

Since Shrey is off visiting his dadi and I'm helping out at Leclair's this weekend, the three of us had agreed to wait until Monday to talk about Micah Demmers and the Tiana/Chavez Elementary connection.

But then Trissa texted me to ask if she could sample Dad's pastries while her mom did her Sunday grocery shopping. How could I say no? For one, my dad's pastries are amazing. For another . . . well, I've profiled forty-eight students this weekend, including my friends. That alone made me guilty enough to say yes.

I wrote out a profile for everyone who could have been the subject of that technology class incident report and everyone I could think of who was a frequent target of bullying, which was no easy feat. I'd even considered *myself* as a suspect. Just to be thorough. However, after thinking long and hard about whether my allergy medicine could cause "sleep bullying," I deduced that I'm probably not the perpetrator I'm looking for.

I swivel to face Trissa and take my notebook out of my large apron pocket, resting it on the counter.

"Okay," I say. "So what did you find out from Tiana?"

"Whoo! Right down to business, I see."

I'm really bad at starting conversations. "Ummmm," I hedge. "How was . . . watching *Rebels*? What did you eat?"

Trissa gives me a scrutinizing look. "*Rebels* was fine, and we ate chow mein and mu shu pork. Is this you trying to chat? Because it's weird. Let's get back to the case."

"Thanks."

Trissa leans in and lowers her voice, even though no one is in the shop at the moment. "I talked to Tiana about Micah, and he could be our new top suspect for *sure*."

"Yeah?"

"Apparently, he cyberbullied a bunch of kids on Tumblr. When the school found out, they asked him to leave."

"Wait, *what?*"

Trissa nods with an all-knowing expression. "Yuh-HUH. He didn't *officially* get expelled, but Micah was 'asked to leave voluntarily for violating the charter rules,' or something. That's what Tiana said at least. Apparently, his Tumblr was mostly filled with mean nicknames, but I guess they're strict about bullying."

"Do you mind if I take a second to write this down?" I ask her, opening the black and white book to one of the last pages. I've filled book #23 at *record* speed, thanks to Ella Baker Shade.

"No, why would I?"

"Shrey hates it when I make my notes and observations when he's there," I explain. "He says it makes me ignore him."

"Okay. I'm gonna try this again. What's with you and Shrey?"

Flushing crimson, I insist, "I told you—nothing! We're friends, and we have been since we were, like, *babies*. Why?"

Trissa fixes me with a knowing look. "You're *always* together. And he stares at you. It doesn't take Nancy

Drew to figure out that there's something more going on there." She waves the remainder of her croissant in my face. "It's obvious."

"You know, funny you should mention Nancy Drew," I say in a rush, desperate to get her off the subject. "Did you know I'm actually named after her? Get it? Nancy Drew . . . *Drew*. My dad's idea. You see, he was never a Hardy Boys fan, but he loved Nancy Drew."

"Nice try," Trissa scoffs. She crosses her legs and leans in. I can't help but notice that, without the restraint of the school's dress code, Trissa has gone all out. Her jacket has sequin happy faces, and her bright yellow shirt features a chibi Princess Leia with a talking bubble that reads INTO THE GARBAGE CHUTE, FLYBOY!

"Nice try what?" I repeat with false innocence.

Trissa narrows her eyes and looks at me searchingly. "Are sure you aren't secretly in love or something? Because we're friends now and you can tell me anything."

"We're not in love!" I cry out louder than I intend to.

Lupe, the cashier for the shop, peeks her head through the doorway from the prep room.

"¿Estás bien?"

Reddening even further, I wave awkwardly. "¡Sí, lo siento, Lupe!"

Trissa won't back down. "Do you want to kiiiissssss him?"

"NO!"

Brrriing!

Thankfully, the jangling of the front door's bell interrupts us. Closing the notebook, I scramble behind the counter, where I'm supposed to be standing watch over the register.

"Excuse me," says a petite curly-haired woman in a sack-style dress.

OBSERVATIONS:

• She has a reusable bag I recognize from our local grocery store, Gino's Farm Fresh Market.

• She also has a personalized tote with a picture of two kids, who look like they're around 8 and 10.

• The older of the two kids looks SUPER familiar. Wait . . . Is that a picture of *Holly Reiss?*

CONCLUSION: Could this be Holly's mom?

"Can I have thirty fruit tarts, please?" the woman asks.

"Sure, ma'am," I say, grabbing an order sheet. "But we only have about a dozen on hand right now. You'll need to preorder that many."

"No problem!" she says.

"If you don't mind my asking," I say, "are you Holly Reiss's mom?"

The woman brightens. "Yes! She's just in the car. Do you know her? Are you friends?" She says the words hopefully, and I wonder how much Holly has told her about school.

"We're new friends," I tell her.

"Holly's awesome!" Trissa adds. "She's such a good artist."

"Oh, I'm glad she's making more friends at school," Holly's mom gushes. "I can't tell you how nice it is to meet you both. Please let me know if you ever want to come over one afternoon. We have an aboveground pool!"

"Sounds good!" I say.

After making the tart order, Holly's mom walks away with a spring in her step, and Trissa and I exchange a long look.

"She sounded surprised that Holly has any friends,"

Trissa says, eyes downcast. "We should reach out to her more."

"We should," I agree. Holly seems nice, and I've always felt like we shared something, because of the reason we were teased at Cypress Grove. Why *haven't* I reached out to her before?

"You know, even before the barfing incident, I had trouble making friends last year," Trissa says suddenly, picking at the remains of her croissant.

I look at her with surprise. Trissa is so friendly and soft around the edges. Unlike creepy and prickly me. It's hard for me to imagine Trissa having trouble making friends.

"Yeah?"

"Yeah. I mean, you kind of had a ready-made friend in Shrey. But all of my friends from Cesar Chavez either went to charter schools or to Skyline Middle. It's just hard to break in, you know?"

"I get it. But you have friends now, right?" I say. "Like Liz, and the kids from your comedy club?"

She smiles. "Yeah. I've got a decent group." Trissa breaks off and beams at me. "I like the friends I'm making now, too."

Regret bowls me over. Did I just make a criminal profile on what could be the only new friend I've made since first grade? Yes, I did. And it makes me feel like a rat. A big, ugly sewer rat who pretends to listen to her friends' problems and then profiles them like a mustache-twirling (rat) villain.

"So . . ." Trissa begins. "Do you think we can catch Ella Baker Shade before fall break? It would be nice to celebrate Halloween triumphant over evil."

"We're going to. I can feel it," I say. I don't mention Dad, or the secret PTO meeting, since I'm afraid that will lead to other confessions.

"Awesome." Trissa stands up and brushes the crumbs from her table and chair into the empty croissant bag. "Okay, I've got to meet back up with my mom at the store. See you Monday, Nancy Drew. Hey, I think I like that even more than Skull Girl!"

"Not an insult; Nancy Drew is great!"

"Okay." Trissa stops short and beams at me. "Hey. I'm really glad I met you, Drew."

The guilt feels like a thousand knives to the gut. Still, I manage to say, "I'm glad I met you too," as she walks out the door.

17

"CAN YOU HELP ME at Leclair's again next Sunday, sweetheart?" Dad asks me a few hours later. We're recovering after a long day, sprawled out on our sectional couch.

"Hmmm. Maybe. If by 'help' you mean binging on marzipan and watching *Forensic Files* on my phone. That sounds okay . . ." I say lazily. I'm *tired*, and clearly Dad hasn't been reading up on child labor laws.

"Watching *Forensic Files without* me?" Dad exclaims in a theatrical tone. "Curse you, Drew Leclair. Curse you *and* your family!"

"*You're* my family."

"Fair point."

Leaning back, I add, "Also, I'm hungry."

Dad throws up his hands. "Fine! I'm ordering food.

Do you want to invite Shrey over tonight? We could watch some movies—"

"No!" I shout, practically flailing off the side of the couch.

"What?"

"I mean . . . no thanks. Casually."

It's too late. Dad squints at me, perplexed. "Did you just say 'casually' to make it sound casual? Because it didn't work. What's going on? Are you and Shrey fighting?"

I close my eyes, letting out a long sigh. What do I do? I can't tell him everything that's been going on—not after all the crying Friday night. But he knows I'm upset about *something*. He doesn't need to worry about Ella Baker Shade, but maybe I could talk to him about the Shrey problem.

I bite my lip, trying to figure out the best way to say it . . .

Hey, Dad. If I'm not interested in kissing boys or girls by the seventh grade, does that mean I'll never be interested in kissing anyone?

Hey, Dad. Does it mean something that I can only imagine being in fictional relationships with fictional characters in a world in which I am also fictional?

Hey, Dad. Is it weird that I crush on both boy and girl characters in said fictional world, but the idea of actually touching my mouth to their mouth is TOTALLY gross?

Nope. Each of these scenarios would find me projectile vomiting all over the living room.

"Drew?" he nudges me, looking worried.

"Fine! Shrey tried to kiss me last week!" I blurt before I can think better of it. "Like, with his *mouth*. And now it's all weird, and we can't do regular Drew and Shrey stuff anymore. I mean, what's wrong with being best friends forever, and texting about buckets, and playing video games for twelve hours straight, and binge watching *Stranger Things*, and . . . Well, there you have it. Shrey tried to kiss me, and now he wants some kind of 'next level' situation, but what makes kissing the *next* level, anyway? So now everything is ruined forever, and you might have to homeschool me. The end."

Dad's mouth forms a little o, and his eyebrows shoot up to his hairline. "Whoa," he says, after he's fixed his cartoonish face. "That's happening now. Oh, man . . ."

"Wait, what? No. It's *not* happening, Dad. Shrey and I are friends."

"On your end, sure. But I have to tell you, this has been simmering for a while."

"Really?"

"Really. Your mom actually noticed it sometime last year, maybe toward the beginning of sixth grade."

"But . . . why?"

Dad sighs heavily and rubs his eyes as if he's suddenly been asked to do a complex equation. "Sweetie, I don't know why. We can't control who we like."

"We can't?" I ask, horrified. "That seems dangerous. What if we end up liking someone who's terrible for us?"

Dad's wry smirk is quick enough that I almost miss it. But there it is. Of course he knows about falling for someone bad. He fell for Mom. And he probably still loves her, too, despite the fact that she's off kissing my guidance counselor in Kauai. *Yurt* kissing, which sounds even more disgusting than regular kissing.

"Ohhhh . . ." I say slowly. "Yeah. So, you really can't control who you like."

Dad looks pained. "Nope."

"But what happens now?" I ask him. "If Shrey can't control who he likes, what am I supposed to do? I don't want to kiss him."

"You sure?"

"Yes, I'm sure!" I snap. "So . . . does that mean something?"

"Do *you* think it means something?"

Suddenly, my face feels hot. I'm sure I'm beet red at this point. "I don't know," I tell him. "I haven't liked anyone real yet."

"Real?"

"Oh, come on. You know what I mean." I may have a closer relationship with my dad than most girls my age, but I'm not ready to go into detail about the fictional characters thing. It's too hard to explain.

"Are we talking about your crush on Han Solo here?"

I exhale, beaming. "Yes! *Thank* you!"

Dad smiles knowingly. "Look, kiddo. You're not even a teenager yet. A lot of kids are thinking about these things, but you might not be there yet. Or . . ." He trails off, clearing his throat and sounding awkward. "Or you might never, and that's okay too. Wherever you end up, that's you. And you're amazing. Okay?"

"Yeah. Thanks." Suddenly I find myself very interested in my hands. My eyes glued downward, I say, "You know . . . Shrey asked me if I was into boys. And, um, I don't only have crushes on boy characters." The confession makes my face go completely hot, and for a moment I wonder if I might melt into the couch.

Dad responds immediately. "If you end up liking girls—or both—that's fine too. But I gotta tell you, that question is less about you and more about Shrey protecting his feelings. It's easier to believe someone is rejecting your whole gender than the truth—you don't want to be with them specifically."

Considering that for a moment, I finally look back up at him. "Would it have been easier for you if Mom had left with some lady instead of Mr. Clark?"

"A little."

I swat an escaped tear from my cheek. "Okay. I think we need to be done talking about this now."

"Phew!" Dad mock-wipes his brow. He reaches forward to give my hand a squeeze, and I squeeze it right back. "So should we order in from Little Hunan?"

"A *hundred* percent yes. Get extra fortune cookies, though."

Thankfully, the rest of the night is dedicated to greasy takeout and *Trail of Blood* instead of my questionable identity. However, when I go to bed a little after ten, the sting of embarrassment from my conversation with Dad is still there. Especially the idea that I might be "too young" to have feelings for people.

Everyone has always pointed out how mature I am. Mostly adults, but still. Being too babyish to have crushes is embarrassing. If I'm so mature, shouldn't *all* of me be maturing at the same speed?

Once I'm safely in my room with the door closed

behind me, I find myself self-consciously typing questions into Google that I would never say aloud. After a lot of reading, a conclusion forms: it's too soon to know whether I'm asexual with any certainty. Also, even if I am, I *could* be interested in romance. Apparently, plenty of people don't start having *Feelings* until well after puberty. Since I haven't started my period yet, maybe my body doesn't have those hormones yet? So, not a maturity thing but a regular old body chemistry thing. Totally out of my control.

I'm about to close my laptop and get ready for bed when I see a notification pop up on my phone. Oof. A new post from Ella Baker Shade:

> which Ella baker bully was caught falling flat on his face? watch the Video and see micah demmers' epic fail! 😊 😊 😊 until next time, from your friendly Neighborhood ella baker shade!

After watching a short, repeating video of Micah Demmers biting it by one of the portables, I turn my attention back to the post itself. Something is off about it. It's almost as if it was written hastily, which seems out of character for Ella Baker Shade. I'm peering at it closer when I start to see the comments flooding in. Most of it is what you'd expect—more laughing emojis and general responses laughing at Micah's fall. But I stop short when I see one comment pop up, from a user named HollsBells that I'm fairly sure is Holly Reiss based on my notes. The comment reads:

Finally he gets what he deserves!

Huh. That doesn't sound much like Holly. Comments begin to flood the feed, and the comment gets pushed up. Quickly, I scroll back to find it again. But, when I get to the spot where it was, the comment is gone. Double-checking, I scroll through each comment, checking new ones that pop up too.

Nothing.

Why would Holly write a comment like that only to immediately delete it?

My mind reels with options. Sure, Holly could have regretted posting a comment and deleted it, but was it more than that? Did she post a comment as herself, and suddenly realize it might link her to Ella Baker Shade?

Could *Holly* be the victim I'm looking for?

18

"HOW MANY PHONES have you confiscated today?" Mrs. Jackson is asking Ms. Woodrich in the staff room the next day.

Like last week with Alicia's post, the whole campus has been watching the "epic fail" video of Micah on repeat. This time, though, the teachers seem to finally be taking notice. As I quietly staple Fall Fest brochures during my TA period, I listen intently to the staff room gossip.

"Twelve," my Core teacher replies with a snort. "This Instagram thing is getting completely out of control. One kid looked like I stole his reason to live when I took it. I told him I'd give him back the phone after school, but, well *you* know. Has anyone talked to Mariam about this?"

I perk up my ears. Mariam is Principal El-Sayed's name.

"Doesn't help that we're still without a counselor," Mrs. Jackson complains. "It's been two weeks since Dustin left, and the district hasn't even posted his position. It's plain nonsense. All I'm saying."

"I'm telling you, there's something in that guy's files," Ms. Woodrich says. "Didn't some kid hack into La'ei's Facebook page? She didn't say who, but they should at least question that kid if someone is cyberbullying. It would be nice to have some answers for the parents this week. I've gotten five emails today alone."

Mrs. Jackson makes a *pshaw!* sound and grabs a stack of papers from the copy machine. "Maybe someone should call Dustin in Hawa—"

Ms. Woodrich puts up a hand to stop her, swiveling to face me with a horrified look.

"Nice work on those packets, Drew!" she says, as if she's trying to pretend the last two minutes didn't happen. She grabs her papers and motions for Mrs. Jackson to follow her out of the staff lounge. "Keep it up, and I'll see you next class, okay?"

Nodding, I give them a wave and then slump over in my chair. When the door closes, I reach into my backpack for my phone. Dismissing a few text notifications from Shrey and Trissa, I go back to the Micah Demmers post. I hate to give it more views by watching it again, but I keep thinking I can decode the language in the post, or see a new clue.

Holly Reiss still seems like the least likely candidate for the Shade. She doesn't fit the profile, and one of the meanest posts had been about her. But might that be a tactic to make her *seem* less guilty? Also, I have zero observations on Holly that make me think she's involved on social media. Before the deleted post, I'd only seen a couple of remarks on the Badgers Insta.

And what Facebook incident was Ms. Woodrich talking about? La'ei is Ms. Tuitasi's name. Was that what the hacking on the report was all about? Holly is in that second period class, too. I'd profiled her with the rest of that period, but I didn't think for a moment she could be the Shade. Maybe I was wrong to eliminate her.

Something tells me I *have* to get that name.

I'm still obsessing on the way to meet Shrey and Trissa for lunch when a chill shoots up my spine, causing my whole body to shudder. I turn my gaze instinctively toward the breezeway by the library. Is someone watching me? Again?

You're getting paranoid, Leclair, I tell myself. *Trissa already said she was the one who was following you that day.*

With great effort, I manage to shake off the weird feeling. I stalk into the library, where I find both my friends in the 000s section.

Trissa looks up from her graphic novel. "Hey!" she says, but then screws up her face with concern. "Everything okay?"

"Yeah. You look weird," Shrey says.

"Everything is fine," I reply. I'm hoping the more times I say it, the faster it will become true. "Just frustrated. It feels like we're so close but can't get at the truth. I did get some information in the staff room today that could be useful, though."

Leaning in, I recount what I overheard, along with my suspicions about Holly.

"I don't know," Trissa says when I finish. "Holly? That doesn't sound right."

"But that comment she made on the Micah post doesn't sound right either," Shrey says. "Maybe we just don't know her very well?"

"True," I say. "But I think Trissa's right, too. It doesn't really make sense with what we know about Holly. I think finding out that name on the incident report might make things clearer—"

Bzzzzzzz! A vibrating notification sounds on my phone.

"Another post?" Trissa moans. "It's only been, like, twelve hours."

"This perp is escalating." I nod.

Shrey jabs me with his elbow. "Maybe you should stop talking like you're on *Criminal Minds*."

"Says the guy who quoted Sokka approximately a thousand times last week," I retort playfully.

Giggling, I move to tap on my Instagram notification, but then I see that it isn't a post at all. It's a message request . . .

. . . from *ELLA BAKER SHADE*.

"Aaaaahhhhh!" I exclaim, tossing my phone on the floor as if the Shade is about to come crawling out.

"What?" Shrey exclaims.

Mr. Covacha peers around the corner. "Everything okay over here?"

"Yes," I say. "Sorry, Mr. Covacha. We'll be quiet."

"Thanks, you three," he says, returning to the checkout desk.

"What is it?" Trissa asks.

I show both of them my phone, and their expressions quickly morph from confusion to horror, like mine.

"Wait, what?" Shrey says in a stage whisper.

"Open it!"

I hesitate for a moment. Ella Baker Shade is sending

messages to me, *personally?* Part of me wants to delete the request. But then I remember my go-to question: *What would Lita do?* If the Junipero Valley Killer had sent notes to her, not just the local papers, would she have thrown them away? Definitely not.

Trissa seems to sense my reluctance. "On three?" she suggests. Both of them are pressed at my back, peering at my phone.

"Okay," I say, wincing. "One . . . two . . . three!"

I press Accept on the request, and three things happen, seemingly in slow motion. First, a photo appears. Then, my chest begins to throb like the wind was knocked out of me. Following this, Shrey and Trissa lift their eyes to look at me with pity.

It's another picture of my mom and Mr. Clark, but this one is worse. *Way* worse.

Avoiding their eyes, I keep my face glued to my phone as I read the caption:

This picture is just for you, Drew Leclair. Looks like Mr. Clark is slipping your mom the tongue — BIG time. Stop asking everyone about Ella Baker Shade, or there's more where this came from and a LOT worse. Next time it's POSTED.

19

BECAUSE I REFUSE TO CRY, my stomach is the thing that gives. After what I hope was a great performance with Shrey and Trissa (pretending that I wasn't upset and convincing them I wanted to question Ms. Tuitasi before class), I end up vomiting in the gender-neutral bathroom outside the library. I barf so many times that I consider heading to the nurse's office. But I don't. If I do that, Ms. Marika will ask me what's wrong. Then she'll tell Vice Principal Lopez. He'll make me give him my phone and will call Dad again, and then everything will come out, ending with that awful picture. It's like this book I read in kindergarten, *If You Give a Mouse a Cookie*, only with a lot more vomit.

When the barfing finally stops, I look at the picture again.

The real gut punch isn't the fact that Mom is wrapped around Mr. Clark like a bikini-clad octopus. Or that she's wearing swimwear that she definitely didn't buy with us at Kohl's or Target. Or the kissing. It's the look on her face.

She's finally free. Happy. Joyful. *Without* us.

How could she do this to us—especially to Dad! She was supposed to love Dad. She was supposed to be my mom. But where is she? Yeah. In a stupid yurt, causing all this mess!

Shifting from my kneeling position, I sit with my back against the tile wall. I can't even muster the energy to think about how gross the bathroom floor is.

Trembling, I retrieve my phone and look at the message again. Another gag reaction hits me when I see the picture, but this time something sticks out about the caption: *Looks like Mr. Clark is slipping your mom the tongue—BIG time.*

Wait—isn't that exactly what Johnny Granday said to me last week? That I was "too busy imagining Mr. Clark slipping Mom the tongue to walk straight"?

I jump up from the floor.

Yes.

That was *exactly* what he said.

Could my profile have been that off base? Are we

not looking at a victim as the perpetrator, but *Johnny* as Ella Baker Shade? I bolt out of the bathroom and step onto the breezeway. Of course, the moment I do, I remember that lunch is over. There's no way to confront Johnny now—especially since I'm late to technology class. Maybe I can catch up with him after school, before I meet up with Shrey and Trissa?

Sighing with resignation, I walk back into the library.

"Drew!" Mr. Covacha says with surprise. "What are you doing here?"

"Um, I was feeling sick," I explain, gesturing toward the bathroom. "Could I possibly get a hall pass?"

"Of course!" he says. But just as he heads for the back room to get the pass, the phone rings. The librarian holds up a finger as if to say *just a minute* and answers the phone with a curt "Covacha here!"

I'm still feeling too jittery from the Granday connection to stand still. So, I wander back toward the 800s, stopping short when I see a familiar face. Seated in the study area, legs slung over one of the cloth chairs, is none other than Ethan Navarez.

"Ethan!" I say. "What are you doing here?"

He's hunched over the desk and sketching when he looks up at me, surprised. "Oh, hey, Drew. Ms. Tuitasi let me come here to work on 'Hour of Code.' Which I guess I should get to." Ethan closes his binder, and something about the image on the front tugs at my mind—a thread to something I can't quite put my finger on. "I'm also in here a lot," he adds. "I have a doctor's note for PE. They let me hang in the library first period."

"I did that all last year," I say. "Asthma."

"Same," he says.

"Nice!" I exclaim, even though it's a weird thing to bond over.

"So," he says. "Any progress with Ella Baker Shade?"

I hesitate. Shrey and Trissa don't even know about Granday shooting back up to suspect #1. I shouldn't blab to Ethan about it.

"Getting closer and closer," I say vaguely.

Ethan looks pleased, and something in the way the corners of his mouth twitch upward bothers me. He's not smiling with relief. He's almost . . . smirking? Narrowing my eyes, I look at him with interest.

OBSERVATIONS:

- Ethan is wearing a standard Ella Baker polo, which makes me wonder if he got dinged on the dress code for that Junipero Valley White Hats logo shirt last week.

- He closed his book as soon as he saw me, a binder that's emblazoned with the same image that won him the 6th-Grade Reflections contest.
- He is making uninterrupted eye contact, as if *he's* observing *me* right now.

CONCLUSION: . . .

Wait.

The yearbook.

If light bulbs actually appeared over people's heads when ideas formed, about a million lights would be popping up right now, one at a time. I glance down at Ethan's binder again, with his "Badgers in Unity" artwork. Then, I glance upward at the large painted Ella Baker Badger mural above the library door. The style is completely different, I realize. The mascots painted around the school are like the Badger images on our student datebooks—a textured and illustrated look with lines, highlights, and shadows. Ethan's image is flat, with bold, solid colors. The digitally precise black outline doesn't look like it was done by hand. The teeth are a clean, looped sweep. It's an almost *exact* replica of the hooded Badger signature on Ella Baker Shade's posts!

The nagging feeling I've been having for days lifts as everything starts to fit. How could I not have seen this? Literally, if you add a hoodie and sunglasses to Ethan's Badger design, it would be identical.

"Drew?" Ethan says. "Are you okay?"

He looks at me, worried. But is he really worried? Or is he trying to figure out if I got his message? The message, I realize, that led me right to *Johnny Granday*. The phrasing about Mr. Clark slipping my mom "the tongue." (Ugh. Still gross.) Wasn't *Ethan* there when Johnny said that to me? I squeeze my eyes shut, recalling the incident last week. Yes. Johnny smacked Ethan as he passed us by. And why does he seem to be everywhere? Could it be that the weird feeling of being watched was Ethan?

"I'm fine," I say, attempting to keep my voice calm. "Just distracted I guess. So . . . do you still think it's Johnny Granday who's been making all these posts?"

"For sure," Ethan says, a little too eagerly. "I can't believe you're, like, investigating Johnny Granday. I hope you get him suspended."

"Mmmm-hmmm."

Ethan's eyes are somehow both dark and gleaming. "Have you found anything on him?"

"I can't talk about that yet," I say, embarrassed to hear my voice quaver. "But I'll let you know as soon as I have proof. Listen, sorry to bail, but Mr. Covacha has a pass for me. See you tomorrow?"

"Count on it." Ethan speaks with a friendly air, but every word he says now sets my hairs on end.

Giving him a (totally casual) wave, I walk back to the library desk, where Mr. Covacha is waiting with the hall pass. My mind races as I take it and head out into the hallway.

Could Ethan Navarez be Ella Baker Shade?

One more point stands out as I recall my observations in the library. That Junipero Valley White Hats shirt last week. It sounded familiar, and not just because of the Junipero Valley Killer. Breathlessly, I duck into the garden behind the library to pull out my phone. I type "Junipero Valley White Hats" into Google, and right away, I see what I need. They are a friendly hacking group, advertising password retrieval for large companies. Companies like Facebook and Instagram.

My memory catches as I remember one more piece: the Micah post. I'd been so thrown off by Holly's deleted comment that I hadn't taken the time to study the post on its own. Opening my Instagram app, I note again the strange style, with random lowercase and capitalized letters. I'd thought maybe Ella Baker Shade had written it in haste. But wouldn't a phone (if that is the weapon of choice) autocorrect those issues? When I look at the words again, I see it:

> which Ella baker bully was caught falling flat on his face? watch the Video and see micah demmers' epic fail! 😄😄😄 until next time, from your friendly Neighborhood shade!

The capital letters. If you put them together, they spell EVN. As in . . . Ethan Victor Navarez.

What?

The light bulbs keep on popping, as I remember what Ms. Woodrich said about a hacking incident and a boy who was so upset about losing his phone. Also, Ethan hadn't been in sixth period technology at the beginning of the year. He only showed up a few weeks ago, at the end of September. Could he have been the subject of that incident report from August? Everything is coming together so seamlessly it almost doesn't feel real. The clues were never leading me to Johnny or Holly. They all lead to—

"Hi, again," Ethan Navarez says softly.

20

IF I COULD LITERALLY JUMP out of my skin, I think I would at this moment. Ethan has sidled up behind me —so close that I wonder if he can see my Google search. "Oof! I mean . . . um, what's up, Ethan?"

He offers me an impenetrable smile. "I just wanted to say thank you. I wanted to before, but I thought it might be weird."

"Thank you?" I manage to repeat. My voice sounds strange, as if drowned out by my own heartbeat.

Ethan goes on: "People complain, but nobody really *acts* when it comes to bullying here. If you bring someone like Granday down—well, it's more than the teachers have done."

"You're welcome?" My face must be frozen in cringe mode right now.

"Well . . . bye!" Ethan's eyes follow me for a moment as he turns, and it reminds me of those creepy portraits in ghost stories. Finally, he disappears back into the library.

I stare after him with determination, willing my pulse to slow so that I can think like a profiler. Ethan certainly seems interested in making me think Ella Baker Shade is Johnny Granday. With that private message that he must have known I would connect to Johnny . . .

There's the motive, I think. Ethan isn't just randomly trolling. He's trying to frame Johnny Granday. And, no matter how much I hate Johnny, I have to stop him.

***

"I don't know, Drew," Shrey says as the three of us walk up the street toward my house. "Ethan Navarez? Really?"

"For the fiftieth time, yes!"

"But he's, like, *super* quiet . . ." Trissa points out.

"And what do people say about *serial* killers?" I ask, wide-eyed.

Trissa laughs. "I don't know what people say. I don't spend all my time watching true crime documentaries."

"They're quiet, nice, keep to themselves," Shrey lists in a dull voice. From the look of it, he's gunning for first prize in sarcastic eye-rolling.

I give him a hurt look. He's heard it all before, I know.

But Shrey has been with me for years. He saw me solve the mystery of the ketchup graffiti last year (Christina and her friends had been writing the stylized "bloody" messages to scare the younger kids). He patrolled the neighborhood with me and *saw* me find that missing rabbit, Sir Hoppington (in the drainage pipe down by the creek). Why can't he roll with it this time? Now that Shrey knows I'm not interested in kissing, is he over me as a person?

It's starting to feel that way.

Looking over at both of them, I can tell they need something. I decide to pull *In the Shadow of a Killer* out from my backpack to drop some Lita knowledge.

"Okay," I begin. "This is from the section titled 'The First Victim.' Lita says that a perpetrator's first victim is really important. Maybe the most important part of the whole investigation! You see, perps often murder people who act as substitutes for others in their lives. Especially moms—*tons* of people murder their moms."

An elderly couple passes us on the street, and their heads swivel like owls toward us, eyes wide with alarm.

"It's for a school assignment!" Shrey calls after them, his face flushing.

"Anyway," I continue in a lower voice, "the first victim is meaningful. *Ethan* was the first victim."

"So, he's a substitution for himself?" Trissa asks. "That doesn't make any sense."

"Aaarrrghh, okay!" I exclaim. I'm getting nowhere with them until I can show them the real evidence—the Badger logo, the Junipero Valley White Hats, the coded post. I know they'll be on board as soon as I can show them each connection. "There's a ton more evidence. Just hold on. I'll show you what I mean."

We head up the steps to my front door, and I unlock it, ushering them inside. "Please come to my bedroom, okay? Now. I need to get the crime board."

Shrey snorts.

"What?" I ask irritably.

He lets out another, even more annoying snort. "Nothing. Just bracing myself for another crime board presentation."

My withering glare could melt glaciers. "Fine. If you don't want to hear about it."

"Drew, come on." Shrey laughs. Then, he says the three most annoying words in the history of the universe: "Take a joke."

"Really? You're saying 'take a joke' to *me*?"

"Drew . . ."

"LOOK, DO YOU WANT ME TO EXPLAIN OR NOT?"

"Fine!" Shrey shouts back at me. "Let's go."

I'm leading them both to my bedroom when suddenly I stop dead in my tracks, blinking in realization. The profiles on Shrey and Trissa are still on my desk. "Actually, why don't the two of you wait in the living room?" I say. "I'll grab it."

I duck into my room. It takes considerable effort not to look at the Obi-Wan Mickey plush with the torn papers underneath. It might as well be a billboard advertising my guilt: "Look under me! Drew Leclair is just like the Junipero Valley Killer, but *worse* because she betrays her friends!"

Trissa, I notice when I return to the living room, has already helped herself to a bowl of cereal the size of her head. Giving me a thumbs-up, she swallows and says, "Okay, Nancy Drew. Let's get this show on the road!"

Shrey gives us an odd look, and Trissa explains, "Drew told me that her dad named her after Nancy Drew. She hates Skull Girl, so . . . new nickname."

"When?"

Trissa shrugs and, after swallowing a huge bite of

Cake Flakes, says, "I went to Leclair's yesterday to get a croissant. That's when we talked about my friend Tiana and the Micah Demmers connection."

Shrey looks between me and Trissa, his eyes dark. "Ah. Got it."

"Anyway," I say, casting a worried look at Shrey. "Let me show you what I mean about Ethan." I prop the crime board up against the fireplace and grab my pointer.

"Ready," Trissa says.

Extending the pointer dramatically, I point to Ethan's notes, along with his smiling school picture. "Friends, this is why I've called you here today. To show you the irrefutable evidence that Ethan Navarez is the Instagram cyberbully known as Ella Baker Shade. As you can see from my notes," I continue, smacking the pointer toward the center of the board, "Fact one: Ethan Navarez fits my initial profile for the Shade. Fact two: he has displayed a bitterness toward the school for not punishing Jonathan Granday. And now for the evidence . . ."

I grab the yearbook from the coffee table where I'd left it. "See! The Badger murals around the school look like paintings, with highlights and brushstrokes. The logo on this yearbook—Ethan's design—is computer made. Solid brown, with a precise, thick black outline. Every point of the Badger's fur is the same. Also, look at the teeth here. The way the mouth curves up, with four distinct teeth, is identical to the hooded Badger with sunglasses that Ella Baker Shade uses as a signature in posts. There's the fact that Ethan was in second period when that technology class incident report took place —he only transferred into sixth period a few weeks ago.

"Oh, yeah!" Trissa exclaims. "I forgot, because a bunch of people got switched around that time."

"Yep," I say with a nod. "I super casually asked Ms. Tuitasi about it after lunch, and she confirmed. Then there's Ethan's shirt. The Junipero Valley White Hats. A quick search told me that the company is a friendly hacking service for password security. As in: if Ethan has an association with the company, he could have the skills to hack passwords. And then there's the coded post!" I shove my phone at both of them, pointing out the solo capital letters that spell Ethan's initials. "If my profile was right, he clearly couldn't help from inserting himself into the posts. It's, like, *classic* Junipero Valley Killer!"

"Whoa," Trissa says, wide-eyed. "That *is* weird. And if Ethan was the hacker, it would be easy for him to get into Mr. Clark's Facebook."

"Precisely!" I exclaim, feeling a little like Sherlock Holmes. "And, like you said, Ethan is quiet and unassuming. It completely tracks that he could slink around unnoticed, getting all those embarrassing videos and pictures."

Shrey makes a sort of *harrumph* noise, kicking off his shoes and putting his stinky feet on the couch. "Ehhh, I don't know. What would be the motive?"

"I think it all comes down to Johnny Granday. Ethan has it out for him."

"Then why not use his super creepy skills to get something embarrassing on Granday and post *that?*"

I tense up at Shrey's use of the word *creepy*, but I shake it off and continue, "Ethan wants to see Johnny Granday get in trouble. He wants justice—he said so himself. What better way to make that happen?"

"I don't know . . ." Shrey says again.

I want to kick him, but I simply shut my eyes and ask, "I think the evidence fits. Why can't you just believe me?"

"Okay, fine!" Shrey relents. "I believe you. But the evidence still isn't . . . What's the word you use?"

"Solid? Irrefutable? Concrete? Substantial? Beyond a reasonable doubt?" I offer, rattling off all of my crime vocabulary.

"Yeah, sure. Any one of those. How do we prove that Ethan is the Shade?"

"Well, that incident report got me thinking. Not just

because Ethan transferred periods," I say. "Lita says that detectives look for more low-level crimes committed by perpetrators to prove that they could be capable of the crime. A prior record is a big part of getting to an arrest. If it is him on the report, he may have been caught for similar issues before this year. If so, it should be in the student files in Mr. Clark's office. I'm thinking we sneak in tomorrow, before Ethan has a chance to frame Johnny. If we have something to connect to the evidence, maybe Principal El-Sayed and Vice Principal Lopez will see it and get him to confess. So, are you two with me?"

"Wait, but wouldn't Mr. Lopez know that we broke in?" Shrey asks nervously.

"We don't have to take the files, we could just take pictures or memorize the information. Then we could claim we heard it around school or something. Look, I'll take the blame if we get in trouble, but I think that if I give them a connection *and* all the evidence, it will come together. We need to get on this *now*."

"Why? To protect Johnny Granday?" Trissa asks incredulously.

"No! I mean . . ."

I trail off, thinking about my dad and the special PTO meeting tomorrow. Maybe it's silly to think that solving this will mean the meeting gets canceled. But what if it does? What if we can bring Ethan to justice and Dad never has to find out anything?

"I just feel like Ethan will have something big planned for tomorrow because it's Fall Fest. You know, a big post for before break?" I blurt, reddening at the lie.

"That does make sense," Trissa murmurs in agreement. "But it still seems like a big risk. What if we don't find anything?"

"I'll be right back," Shrey announces in response, heading for the hallway. He's obviously bailing for the bathroom as an excuse to get out of my file room plan, but whatever.

"You guys seem weirder than usual," Trissa whispers as soon as he's out of the room. "Is everything okay?"

Unconvincingly, I stare down the hall and murmur, "Yeah, everything is fi—"

"SERIOUSLY, DREW?" a booming shout erupts from the end of the hallway.

Wait. Isn't Shrey in the bathroom? Why would he be all the way back . . .

"My room!" I jump to my feet. Launching myself full speed, I run down the hall. I come to a skidding halt at my doorway, nearly sliding to a fall due to my socks on the hardwood floors.

OBSERVATIONS:

- Shrey is standing over my desk, next to the toppled-over Obi-Wan Mickey plush.
- He holds two papers.
- The papers are rough at the edges—as in *ripped out*—from a notebook.

CONCLUSION: SHREY FOUND THE PROFILES!

"Why are you snooping in my room?" I move toward Shrey, but he puts up a hand.

"I was getting Jedi Mickey," he says, "not snooping in your room. We got this together, remember? I thought it would lighten the mood to 'use the Force to help us decide our next move.' Are you for real with this?" he asks in a sharp voice, looking down at the profile. "This is *me*."

I blink back tears, trying my best to sound offhand as I reply, "Well, um, of course it's you. And Trissa, and *me* by the way. I profiled pretty much everyone in our class. Remember, you're the one who sent me that class roster with your names on it. Lita says that the only way to eliminate suspects is to track every lead."

"'Lita says.' I'm so tired of hearing that," Shrey says

with a humorless laugh. "You must have known that this was messed up, or you wouldn't have hidden our profiles when the rest of them are probably still in your notebook. Right?"

"I was only—"

"It's funny. What was it you *just* said to me?" Shrey interjects, "Oh, yeah . . . *Why can't you believe me?* I mean, even though the Ella Baker Shade profile sounds like you, I never actually thought it *was.*"

"Wait," I say, backpedaling. But it's too late. Shrey angrily hands over one of the sheets to Trissa, who stands behind us in my doorway.

Shakily, Trissa reads her profile, "'Suspect might be pretending to forge a bond with the profiler in order to deflect guilt from herself'?" She steps back as though I've hit her. She looks hurt. *Really* hurt. "*Seriously,* Drew? That's what you think?"

"No! It's not what I think, I swear! I was only trying to . . . leave no stone unturned."

"So, have you suspected me, like, this whole time?" Trissa asks, looking so sad that a pang of guilt tightens around my chest until my breath comes out in a wheeze.

"Of course not," I exclaim, tearing up fully at this point. Sucking in a jagged breath, I look around the room to find a focus. Nothing.

"Well then, what is this?" Trissa asks.

"It's just, well, we weren't getting anywhere, and . . ." I try to force myself to tell them about Dad, and how worried I am about him, but the explanation dies in my throat. "Ummm, I figured I needed to speed up the investigation and do some work on my own."

"By profiling your friends?" Trissa cries, crumpling the paper and throwing it onto the floor. "Nice. I should have known when you started accusing Holly, I guess. You just suspected *everyone*, and used us to help you narrow the list. I've got to be honest, this hurts. Especially after I told you how it feels when adults do that to me all the time."

"Trissa—"

"No. I'm gonna go grab a bus," she says, giving me one last hurt look. "I thought that we were actually becoming friends. Was all of that because you wanted to catch me doing something?"

"No! I mean, yes, we are friends! Trissa, wait . . ."

For a second, I think Trissa might stop. But she simply turns her head, closing my bedroom door on the way out. Trissa's soft footsteps retreat down the hallway, and then I hear the door shut behind her. For a moment I think Shrey is going to bail too, but he stands rooted to his spot by my desk.

"I can't believe you did this," he says darkly. "Are you *that* much of a robot? It's like you can't *see* us at all, or how this would make us feel."

I start to feel heat behind my eyes as the tears spill out, one by one. "I—I'm sorry, Shrey. I really never thought it was you or Trissa, I swear. It's just that you have to be thorough if you want to solve a—"

"Solve a crime?" Shrey guesses with an acidic tone. "Drew. We are in the *seventh grade*. We're supposed to be playing video games and kissing and . . . telling each other things. You know, stuff like the fact that I'm a *suspect in your profiles!* But you never tell me how you're feeling. You just make a joke or change the subject. And I'm tired of—" He breaks off, shaking his head. "You know what, *no*. Trissa had it right. I'm out of here."

"Fine!" I yell after him. "Just leave, then! I don't need your help, anyway. Go hit a ball or something. Go make some other best friend and make sure to never mention your collector's edition wands or your Appa stuffed animals. Or your math joke books or your grief about Pluto losing planet status, which happened, like, before you were *born*."

"Fine!"

"FINE."

He slams the door on his way out, and I sink to the

floor, tears streaming down my face. I think about the picture Ella Baker Shade sent me of Mom, the smile on her face and the sun kissing her freckled skin. Then, I wonder: what will Shrey's life be without me?

Probably a lot better.

He'll probably have a new best friend who loves sky bison *and* baseball within a week because he's not— what did he call me again?

A *robot*.

But not a nice one, like WALL-E. A mean one, like that evil steering wheel from *WALL-E*. A robot who writes terrible, hurtful things about her friends when they did nothing but help. Squeezing my eyes shut, I imagine a picture of Shrey, post-Drew: a happy, smiling face laughing with his baseball or basketball team. Then I let myself ask the question I've been avoiding for over a week:

What is it about me that makes everyone want to leave?

21

SO MUCH FOR THINKING like a scientist.

By the time Dad texts me that he's heading home, my soft crying has become earth-shattering sobs. Soon, I'm sucking in air and gasping, a high-pitched noise coming out with each attempt. Great. The asthma is back for an encore.

Though it hurts to breathe, I pull myself up and stumble to the hallway bathroom, where I grab a penguin-shaped breathing nebulizer from the closet. I haven't used it in a year, and the medical solution has probably expired, but whatever, I can't feel any worse. After a few minutes, my sobbing forces me to take deep breaths, and I finally feel the vapor from the medicine reach my lungs. When the nebulizer starts to make a loud sucking noise, I toss the empty mouthpiece to the floor, still crying but also noticeably shakier from the treatment.

Everything is such a mess right now.

Trudging back to my room, I collapse onto my bed, pulling a pillow under me. Without thinking, I grab my notebook, flipping through my observations from the past few weeks. As I read my notes on Trissa and Shrey, my breathing starts to slow. All through this investigation, they've been there. Trissa, relating to each of the victims with empathy and ease. Shrey, having the courage to question Johnny Granday. They've been backing me up this whole time. And Trissa wasn't wrong. Writing a profile on her after she told me all that stuff about feeling like she's being watched by teachers was totally messed up. It may not be as bad as the stuff Micah Demmers says, but it cut her just the same.

Their words echo in my memory—too loud for me to shut out.

I refused to believe them without the evidence to back it up, I realize. I was trying so hard to be like Lita, that I forgot to be what they needed me to be—a good friend. Shrey and Trissa didn't leave because I'm weird. Didn't Shrey say he *likes* me because of those things?

And Trissa—didn't she say she was glad she met me? This couldn't all be because I'm creepy.

No. This happened because I messed up.

And I need to make it right.

Instinctively, I grab for my notebook. What if I update the profile I made of myself and show it to them? Would that make them see how sorry I am?

Still shaky, I scribble:

OFFENDER PROFILE

NAME: Drew Leclair

AGE: 12 **RACE:** White

EYES: Green **HAIR:** Auburn Brown

KNOWN ALIASES: Fatface, Skull Girl, Nancy Drew, Special Agent Drew Leclair (someday)

VICTIMS:

~~None.~~

1) Shrey, 12: friend, sportsman, nerd, and skilled fartbender.

2) Trissa Jacobs, 12: friend, comedienne,
Jedi knight of the highest caliber.

***

No. An offender profile is something *I* would appreciate, not my friends. Isn't that what Shrey had said? That I was too busy obsessing about solving crimes to see them? That I shut them out?

"I'm the *worst*," I mutter. The half-written profile seems to stare back at me as if in agreement, so I shove it away angrily. How is it possible that everything fit so perfectly just hours ago and now nothing makes sense?

Even my plan to catch Ethan seems far away from me now. Trissa was right: breaking into the student files *is* a big risk when I'm not even sure that Ms. Tuitasi's report is about Ethan. Or if he's been caught for anything before. Is it worth maybe getting suspended just to keep Dad from finding out about the posts?

Not even Lita Miyamoto can help me now, I realize as I flip through *In the Shadow of a Killer*. There's plenty about how to catch a serial killer but pretty much zero on how to apologize to your friends. And this apology has to come from *me*.

I grab for my notebook again and begin to write, tears dripping onto the lined pages of my notebook.

> I know you're not speaking to me right now and I deserve that. I can't believe I made those profiles. It was a horrible and nasty thing to do. I completely broke your trust when you've been nothing but amazing friends and I'm sorry.

Once I start, the words come faster and faster.

> Shrey, you've been my rock since first grade. You were friends with me when no one else would come near me with a ten-foot pole. You are hilarious, and nerdy in the best way. You say I'm always loyal to you, but it's easy because you're literally the best. I love watching you play sportsball, even though I don't get it, because I like seeing you happy. You deserve everything good in this world, and I totally betrayed that because I was so worried that you wanted me to be someone different.
>
> Trissa, I never thought I would have another friend in my whole life. But then you came along, and you're one of the coolest people I've ever met. You

manage to be fun and kind, too, which is impressive. You are exactly as awesome as Ahsoka Tano, and you KNOW how awesome that makes you. I blew it by being a full-on traitor. I'm so glad we became friends too, and I hope you can forgive me.

The truth is, this hasn't just been about solving a mystery for me. I've been so afraid that my dad will break down and I decided I would do anything to keep him from finding out about the posts. There's a lot I haven't told you about my mom, and how things are now. I worry that Dad will be sad forever. I worry that she left home because I'm not who she expected. I wish I'd just *told* you instead of hurting you by trying so hard to keep it together.

Wet spots blur the black ink in sections of text, but I don't even care anymore. I write down everything that happened, from Mom leaving, to her letters, to me being afraid that Dad would find out about all of it at the PTO meeting this week. When I'm done, I take pictures of the letter and text them each image, one by one.

"Hey, honey!" Dad calls out just as I've placed my phone down on the desk.

Wiping my face with my sleeve, I manage to shout, "Hi, Dad! Be right out, okay?"

I'm not sure if Shrey and Trissa will forgive me, but one thing is starting to feel clear again: I have to catch Ella Baker Shade. Ethan was cruel to Holly, Connor, and Trissa. He posted about my family not once but *twice*. And, even though I know I messed things up (maybe forever), he's the one who started hurting people.

My friends shouldn't have to risk getting in trouble, but that doesn't mean I shouldn't try, even if it's just a chance. Or else what's the point of everything that happened today?

I need more than a profile. I need a plan.

22

DREW'S MEGA-SECRET PLAN (FOR MY EYES ONLY!)

STEP ONE: Wait for Ms. Marika to take her coffee break during my TA period in the office. Get the "Fall Fest!" flyers that Ms. Marika asked me to put up for the event.

STEP TWO: Convince the counseling center secretary, Mr. Crohner, to offer to put up "Fall Fest!" flyers up around campus using Leclair charm and previous observations of Mr. Crohner as a fitness nut (see: frequently drinks protein

shakes, observed viewing high-intensity
interval training videos).

STEP THREE: Find Ethan's file, and
hopefully priors that will help me
convince Vice Principal Lopez that Ethan
is the troll. Memorize or take pictures.
STEP FOUR: Go to Mr. Lopez with all
the evidence. At which point Ethan will
hopefully be exposed as the evil genius
he is.

"Drew!" Dad calls from the kitchen. "Are you ready
for school? I made pancakes! And I don't want to micro-
wave the syrup *again!*"

"Okay, Dad! Be right there!" I shout back. Glancing at myself in the mirror, I realize that I look like I'm
headed for any day at school. Well . . . maybe not any
day. Since Fall Fest is this afternoon, the dress code is
holiday-relaxed, and we have more breathing room for
self-expression.

I've opted for black leggings with my most school-
friendly *Crime and Waffles* shirt. It's super cute — a
cartoon waffle with the faces of the hosts, Karrie and
Grace, in the center. I added a denim jacket and the
quintessential accessory for any covert mission: a plain

black beanie. Nancy Drew wears them on the new CW show. It's clearly the I'm-about-to-break-and-enter-but-I'm-still-the-hero look.

"Hey!" Dad says in surprise when I walk into the kitchen. "Where's your costume?"

"Huh?" I look down at my *Crime and Waffles* shirt and then realize what he means. "Ohhh. My real costume is for *Halloween*, not school," I tell him with a wave. "Nobody wears costumes at school."

Dad screws up his face sadly. "Sounds like seventh grade is the end of Halloween fun," he says as he takes out his phone.

"Not for us!" I reply a bit too eagerly.

I'm trying *not* to look like a kid who's about to violate school property. He doesn't notice the look on my face, thank goodness.

When Dad heads to his room to get ready and I hear the shower turn on, I hastily return to my room to make sure I have everything I need for the file heist. First, I check my crime board, unpinning my notes on Ethan and placing them in my backpack. Then, I double-check the plan. Ducking out on Ms. Marika will be easy, but Mr. Crohner might be more of a wild card. If I can get past him, I can slip into Mr. Clark's old office and . . .

Wait. What if the office is locked? I need to be prepared for anything.

Tucking the crime board away, I grab my phone, and type the words "picking a lock" into Google. I manage to ignore the glaring absence of texts from Shrey or Trissa, clicking on a Reddit thread on lock picking.

My nerves are still getting the better of me at the idea of breaking into school property, but isn't it for a good cause? Besides, Nancy Drew has her own lock-picking kit to go with her mission beanie, and she's definitely in the "good guy" camp.

Before Dad finishes his shower, I dart into the kitchen for my supplies: a handful of paper clips and a plastic Diet Coke bottle from the recycling bin. Following the subreddit's instructions, I cut a few rectangular pieces out from the plastic and slip them into my backpack along with the paper clips.

A few minutes later, when we get in the car, Dad puts on the new episode of *Crime and Waffles*. But I can't focus on whatever murder they're talking about. When I can't pay attention to a *true crime* podcast, you know something is wrong. For the first time in a long time, the school day can't come fast enough.

***

HAVE A BALL AT FALL FEST!
REMEMBER: NO CLOWNS!

The office reeks of pumpkin spice when I arrive for third period (a.k.a. heist zero hour!) and Ms. Marika immediately shoves a thick stack of Fall Fest flyers into my hands. I smirk as I look down at the epic list of "Fall Fest DON'TS," which are mostly clown-related.

Since this murderous clown scare a few years back, all the Oakland schools freaked out and changed everything from "Halloween" to "Fall Fest." As I recall, there were no actual murderous clowns. But it's one of those urban legends that just takes hold. I *love* those legends.

Just as I'm starting to distract myself with thoughts of clowns, and coulrophobia, which is a phobia of clowns, Ms. Marika speaks up.

"Are you ready to hang some flyers, sweetheart? I need all the help I can get!"

Giving her a thumbs-up, I drop my backpack behind the attendance desk. "Yes. Those clowns must be stopped!"

Ms. Marika lets out a hearty laugh. "Oh, Drew. You're my favorite. You know that?"

Guilt hits me like a knife to the gut, but I still manage a smile. "That's because I'm the best!" I joke. Feeling guilty reminds me of Shrey and Trissa all over again, so I turn my back and sneakily check my phone again.

Nope. Nothing.

At 10:45 on the nose, Ms. Marika cranes her neck to look at the staff lounge. Right on time. "Hmmmm. I think I'll grab a coffee, dear. Would you mind putting these up around campus while I'm gone?"

I try to hide my excitement. "Sure!" I pick up the large stack of flyers. "All right, then. Enjoy your coffee. I'll be back in a bit."

She gives me a completely nonsuspicious wave, and I once again find myself grateful that adults trust me automatically. The timing could not be working out more perfectly. It's time!

"Duh duh DUHHHH!" I hum a little sneaky detective riff as I head down the hallways to help soothe my nerves. It sounds a little like my dad's old British crime shows, with a dash of the *Incredibles* score thrown in.

"Hello, Drew," Mr. Crohner greets me when I duck into the counseling office. "Was that you I heard? What were you singing?"

"Oh, I was just humming . . ." I break off desperately, realizing that I have no idea what a regular old twelve-year-old girl would listen to. Trissa's into some K-pop band whose name is eluding me. And Shrey likes Ariana Grande. Although I think he's more into her outfits than her music . . .

"Ariana Grande!" I blurt.

"My daughter loves her!"

Ha! "Mission: act casual" is a success!

"So, how are you liking running the desk here in the counseling center, Mr. Crohner?"

"I'm liking it fine!" he says. "Although it's a little quieter since Mr. Clark left." The easy way he says the name makes me think that Mr. Crohner hasn't been partaking in the faculty gossip. Or if he is, he's great at hiding it.

"I bet it's different from coaching, though. Are you still coaching basketball? I'll bet you get a lot of exercise doing that," I say. "I guess that's the real downside of working in an office. So much sitting."

Mr. Crohner takes the bait, frowning. "That is true. The season hasn't started yet, and I have to admit I've been sitting around more than I'd like."

"Well, hey!" I exclaim, as if the idea has just pre-

sented itself. "Why don't you help me put up these flyers? We could split up and get it done in half the time.
You could get some fresh air, and maybe fewer clowns in
your office later!"

Mr. Crohner stands, pushing his chair back and
sucking in his gut. "Let's do it. I've got my walkie-talkie
if any students need to come down to the office. You're
a smart kid, Drew."

We head outside, but as soon as I see Mr. Crohner
heading for the STEM building, I double back to the
student center.

Easing my hand into the pocket of my jacket, I
feel for the jumbo paper clips and the sharp edges of
the plastic rectangles I cut out. As it turns out, I don't
need them. When I peer into the darkened counseling
office on the far end of the student center (which still
has DUSTIN CLARK on the nameplate, by the way), I press
down on the handle and—success!

I slip into the room and close the door behind me.
Zeroing in on the file cabinet in the back of the room, I
creep over and open the top drawer. *A* through *G*. Nope.
However, the next drawer has *H–N*. Ha! My fingers flip
rapidly through the files until I find Ethan Navarez toward the back.

Excitedly, I open up the file and scan it:

INCIDENT REPORT

NAME: Ethan Navarez
SOURCE OF REFERRAL: La'ei Tuitasi
DATE OF REFERRAL: August 28
REASON FOR REFERRAL: Ethan was caught logged in to La'ei Tuitasi's Facebook account with a stolen password, and admitted to logging in to other staff social media accounts as well. Ethan apologized and explained that he was just curious about his teachers.
OUTCOME: Three days of after-school enrichment on digital safety is recommended. Ms. Tuitasi declined to report this to authorities as it was a first offense. She has offered to keep an eye on Ethan and get him involved in other digital activities so that this remains a one-time incident. Ethan has been warned that future activity can and will result in an official report.

"Okay," I murmur aloud. Not exactly a smoking gun, but it's better than nothing. Ethan is hardly the first student to hack into a teacher's social media, but the report connects him to the post about my mom and Mr. Clark at least.

My thoughts trail off, unfocused, as I move back toward the file cabinet and stare at the *H–N* drawer. I'd seen Mr. Clark a bunch of times. The *L*'s should have files on *me*, right? Shifting nervously, I check my phone. Just a few more minutes until Mr. Crohner will be back. That's not accounting for the time I need to leave Ethan's file on Mr. Lopez's desk. As curious as I am to read my file right now, I don't have the time. Do I?

Well, no, obviously. But I still flip through hungrily until I reach my name. It's not, like, Johnny *Granday* thick, but I notice that it's thicker than Ethan's. First up is an incident report from last year:

INCIDENT REPORT

NAME OF STUDENTS(S): Drew Leclair, Christina Bronsky
SOURCE OF REFERRAL: Jillian Radovitch
DATE OF REFERRAL: March 8
REASON FOR REFERRAL: Christina Bronsky confronted Drew Leclair during sixth-grade lunch period, claiming that Drew

was "following her and her friends
around." Christina moved to shove
Drew, and both were brought to the
office. Drew presented handwriting
samples, along with photos she had
taken of Christina writing messages
on the language arts building's walls
in ketchup. When questioned, Christina
admitted to the recurring threatening
graffiti intended to "look like blood."

"Ahhhhhh, yes." I say wistfully, recalling the incident, which I call "Drew Leclair and the Mysterious Condiment Vandal."

I scan through a few more notes, mostly by Vice Principal Lopez, about students complaining that I'm staring at them. Which is a little surprising. I mean, I thought nobody noticed me at all.

Biting my lip, I scan through the rest of last year's notes until I see a handwritten note stapled to the back of my student file. Wait. Are these notes on my counseling sessions? I thought Mr. Clark only kept those digitally for privacy. Ignoring a pit in my stomach that tells me I'm crossing a line, I swallow hard and I read the first line:

Ugh, "recent meeting?" Is that code for making out in his Subaru Impreza? Which is, by the way, *BEIGE* in color?

Mrs. LeClair detailed that Drew has trouble connecting emotionally at home as well as in school. This is in keeping with recent sessions. While Drew does display some antisocial tendencies, however, she seems to self-isolate more than lash out. Mrs. LeClair stated that it was difficult to establish a maternal bond with her daughter due to these tendencies.

Wait, *what?*

Mrs. LeClair has requested regular sessions, since the family is not currently able to afford mental health coverage as small business owners. Hopefully, if counseling sessions are a success, Drew can begin to connect socially with her peers, and at home.

Pressing my eyes shut, as if it will erase the words in front of me, I slam the file down on the desk. So. She thinks it's *my* fault that we don't have a connection? It's *my* fault that she can't act like a regular mom?

Shaking, I pull my phone out of my pocket and scroll down to the *M*'s in my contacts. And there she is. A well-aimed selfie with pouting lips, wearing her Leclair's Eclairs shirt and a messy bun. She doesn't even look like someone's mother.

Well . . . Dad *did* say I needed to call her.

I smash my finger on her icon, pressing the phone button to call. After four agonizingly long rings, her voicemail picks up. Makes sense. Mom's probably too busy jumping off of waterfalls in Kauai right now to worry about whether I'm calling her back.

"Hey, *Mom*. It's your daughter, Drew. Remember me? You're probably swinging in a hammock or doing water yoga now. Whatever *that* is. Well, just wanted to let you know I got your message . . ."

I see a dark shape approaching through the frosted glass on the counseling office door, but I don't care. I'm on a roll now.

"Dad said I should call you. Remember Dad? Yeah, he's the one who's taking care of me now. Did you know that your disgusting pictures from Kauai are all over Mr. Clark's Facebook, and that EVERY STUDENT AT SCHOOL has seen them?"

"Drew," Mr. Crohner says. I spin around to see the muscular secretary walking toward me, a worried look in his eyes.

"Yep. Your cute couple pics are all over school now. I hope you're happy, Mom. Because Dad's not. And I'm not. Which isn't my fault, by the way. I know what you think—that I'm weird and not at all the daughter you expected. But that's *me*, Mom. And you're supposed to love me no matter what. It's *literally* your job."

"Drew, please. Mr. Lopez is on his way. We only want to talk to you—"

"I have all the evidence I need right here in your boy-friend's files!" I spit out the words, and it feels good. "Evidence that it's *not* me. It's you. You're the one ruining everything. So, bye forever, I guess. I hope you and your YURT are very happy together WITHOUT US!"

Tossing my phone to the ground, I look over at Mr. Crohner, then back to the open files on Mr. Clark's old desk. Finally, I turn back to the door, where the looming frame of Vice Principal Lopez has just appeared, next to Principal El-Sayed.

"Drew," Mr. Lopez says in a deep, calm voice. "Please come with me."

23

"PLEASE, SIT DOWN," Mr. Lopez says to me after we enter his office and close the door. Principal El-Sayed sits off to one side, regarding me with genuine concern. "We don't need to talk about the files right now. All we need to know is that you're okay."

The anger that had bubbled up in my chest is rapidly being taken over by nerves—especially under the gaze of the vice principal *and* the principal. So I decide to channel the one girl I know could handle this. *Nancy Drew.*

"I'm f-fine," I say shakily. Completely *un*like Nancy Drew. "I mean . . . I'm *fine*."

Still nervous, I look around the room and make random notes to calm myself down:

OBSERVATIONS:

- Vice Principal Lopez has a picture of a young boy (eight or nine?) in a softball uniform.
- Principal El-Sayed's hijab has cute little ghosts on it.
- A small candy dish sits on Mr. Lopez's desk, but the candy looks old—as if no one has touched the bowl in months.

I snap back to attention when Mr. Lopez says, "Drew. We will eventually want to discuss what happened."

"We don't have to talk about the phone call," I say. Getting the Nancy Drew tone right is hard, but I keep trying. "What I would like to, um, *discuss*, is that a perpetrator is loose on this campus. A perpetrator who is planning another attack any moment."

My voice finally evens out as I roll with the Nancy Drew vibe, and it feels good. In fact, I'm starting to feel as cool as a cucumber.

Well, until Vice Principal Lopez gives me the I'm-not-buying-it look. So, maybe five seconds of cucumber coolness.

"I've asked Ms. Marika to call your father, Drew," Lopez says slowly.

Hot cucumber, hot cucumber!

"She *called* him? He's coming here?"

"I believe so, yes."

They called *Dad*. Which means he's going to find out about everything. Not only me breaking into Mr. Clark's office, but the photos, Ella Baker Shade—

"Can you tell us why you were looking at these files? Was it because of this 'perpetrator' you mentioned?" Principal El-Sayed asks, breaking her silence. "I have to tell you, Drew, I'm surprised. I would never believe that you of all the students here would be caught violating school property."

"I think it's safe to say that you were looking at your file," Lopez offers. "But why Ethan Navarez? Does it have anything to do with this Ella Baker Shade person?"

My butt is officially sweating now. Also, I think I might puke again.

"Okay," I say, in a voice barely above a whisper. "I went into Mr. Clark's office to see if I could find proof that Ethan is Ella Baker Shade."

"Can you tell us *why* you think that?" Principal El-Sayed asks.

I take a deep breath, resting a hand on my arm so I don't start shaking again. "Since last week, I've been trying to profile some of the likely suspects on campus. Ethan wasn't one of them at first, but then a bunch of stuff started to come together . . ." I quickly detail the investigation, leaving Shrey and Trissa out of it, and keeping the focus on Ethan's slipups. "He was caught hacking into teacher social media accounts," I press on. "Just like Ella Baker Shade did with Mr. Clark's Facebook page. He has a T-shirt for Junipero Valley White Hats, which I found out is a *password-hacking* security company. And look at this post about Micah Demmers!"

"Okay," Ms. El-Sayed says.

I hold up my phone, tracing the capital letters to show Ethan's initials, and go on: "Then, there's the Ella Baker Shade calling card—a small signature image he puts on each post. Our murals around the school have a uniform painted style, but the Ella Baker Shade Badger with a hoodie and sunglasses matches Ethan's yearbook design *exactly.* There's also a personal message I got from Ella Baker Shade that used language meant to frame Johnny Granday, who Ethan has been insisting I investigate. Anyway, I know the evidence is circumstantial, but there's a lot of it. I made a crime board to connect everything and it all fits. I *swear.*"

I let out a long breath, during which time Lopez and Principal El-Sayed exchange the world's most confused look.

"You made a *crime* board?" the vice principal sputters.

"And why would Ethan need Johnny to get in trouble for the posts?" Principal El-Sayed knits her brow, perplexed. "I've never seen them fighting . . ."

Summoning all my courage, I blurt, "Okay, can I be honest? One of the reasons I felt the need to investigate these posts is that I don't always feel safe here. Johnny harasses people all the time, and he never gets in trouble for it. And Alicia Alongie. And Micah Demmers. Johnny is really bad, though. Have you noticed that Holly Reiss has gone to the counseling office twenty-five out of fifty-seven days of school this year? I have notes on it. That's mostly Johnny's doing. But when anyone gets upset or fights back, *they* end up with detention, too. It's not fair that the punishment for standing up for yourself is the same as the one for bullying people." I almost open my mouth to detail the pie charts I've made about unequal detention rates, but I decide against it. I'm already in enough trouble.

Both Mr. Lopez and Ms. El-Sayed look taken aback. Lopez levels me with a scrutinizing look and says, "Okay.

That's very fair, Drew. We'll have a conversation with Mr. Granday. And the others."

My whole body is shaking now, partly from fear and partly from the adrenaline produced talking to the principal like that. "Look," I say. "I only want to see Ethan brought to justice. I know he's the anonymous poster. And if you'd let me prove it, I think you'd agree with me."

"Well, that's just it, Ms. Leclair," Principal El-Sayed tells me, leaning in. "We're trying our best to find this person even though the account is not affiliated with the school. But we simply can't let a student . . . investigate other students. What you did today was a massive violation of privacy, whether or not Ethan is the one responsible. Those are student files, and they're confidential. Can't you see that?"

I swallow, hard.

The truth is, I didn't see that. Sure, I feel guilty about breaking into the office and lying to Ms. Marika and Mr. Crohner. But I didn't really consider what it all meant. It even felt wrong to read that note from my own counseling session with Mr. Clark. Sure, I was looking for proof in incident reports, but those notes were so private. How would I feel if someone else snooped in my file and read that about *me?*

All this time I've been focusing on bullies as if there

are only two types of people: bad and good. Your Lita Miyamotos and your Junipero Valley Killers. But what does that make me? I'm the one who profiled my friends when I *knew* that they were innocent. I'm the one who follows people around and takes notes about them. And I'm the one who broke into Mr. Clark's office. Am *I* bad? Or have I been so obsessed with those extremes that I couldn't see everything in the middle? Other than the mean posts, how am I any different from Ethan?

"Drew? Can you see that?" Principal El-Sayed repeats.

"Yes, I can. And I'm really sorry," I say in a thick voice. I pull one sleeve of my jacket down and wipe an errant tear.

"Okay," Vice Principal Lopez says. He looks at the principal, and then they both look back at me. "We'll have to consider what kind of punishment will be appropriate for your conduct today."

"But we're also concerned," Principal El-Sayed continues, in a much softer tone. "When Mr. Crohner heard you in Mr. Clark's office, he said you were screaming into your phone—about your mother and Mr. Clark. Now, I don't know much about what happened there, but I do know that you had some other students laugh at you last week because of that post."

I let out a snotty laugh that sounds anything but funny. "Yep. Not only did my mom leave us, she left with Mr. Clark. The school counselor. Who was, by the way, giving me *guidance* on how best to connect with my mother. You know—the one who left with him. They've been together for months, apparently. He took all these notes . . ." The tears come full force and, this time, I don't bother to stop them.

Mr. Lopez knots his brow for a moment, and then looks me in the eye. "Drew. Are you saying that this relationship started *while* Mr. Clark was counseling you?" He reaches for the file on his desk that reads *Leclair, Drew,* and I watch his eyes scan the page. After he finishes, he lowers his eyes and hands the file to the principal.

"Drew, if this is true, it's very serious for Mr. Clark," Principal El-Sayed tells me, giving Lopez a sideways look like, *Did you know about this?*

"Wait, what?"

The principal takes a deep breath, telling me, "Counseling a student while having a personal relationship with that student's family member. Well, all I can say is that it could have serious ramifications for—"

"That's probably all we should say at the moment,"

Vice Principal Lopez says, pointedly eyeballing me. The principal nods.

"Drew," Vice Principal Lopez says, clasping his huge hands in front of him on the desk. "You're obviously going through something that neither of us can imagine. You will need to be punished, but we're willing to limit that to a two-day in-school suspension. You can collect your bag from the office and wait until your father arrives. I hope the two of you can work this out together."

So, that's it. All of this has been for nothing. Not only did I *not* catch Ella Baker Shade, I failed in my first objective—to keep Dad out of it.

Picturing a full week of ominous glasses cleaning, I realize it will all be on *him*. He'll have to deal with all of this Mom stuff while having a disgraced daughter. How is he going to react when he finds out that I've been keeping it all a secret from him?

Standing from my chair, I nod glumly and turn toward the door. I'm about to leave when I hear a commotion and see two shadows appear on the other side of the frosted glass.

"No! We need to see the vice principal *now!*"

Wait. Is that . . . Shrey?

"Please let us in," another voice pleads. *Trissa?*

"Give that back!" a third voice yells.

What on earth is going on?

After a few seconds, the door bursts open to reveal Trissa and Shrey, looking totally freaked out. When the third figure pushes through, trying to grab something from Shrey, I see why.

Looking at all three of us, eyes blazing with contempt, is *Ethan Navarez.*

24

"HE TOOK MY PHONE!" Ethan accuses hotly, pointing at Shrey.

For a few seconds, nobody speaks.

Then, Principal El-Sayed locks on to Shrey, giving him a Look. "Give it to me," she says calmly. The principal holds a hand out, and Shrey dutifully hands her the unfamiliar iPhone.

Vice Principal Lopez puts up two hands. "Okay. What *happened*?" Both Shrey and Ethan start talking at the same time, so he puts his hands up again. "Ethan, you go first."

Ethan, who has been eager and pleasant for the past few weeks, wears an expression intense enough to equal a *thousand* Death Star explosions. "This guy took my phone," he spits, gesturing to Shrey again.

"Only because of what I saw!" Shrey protests.

"Mr. Malhotra, we'll get to you," Principal El-Sayed says sharply. She turns to Ethan, a crease forming between her eyebrows. "Ethan, can you please be more specific?"

Ethan shifts uncomfortably. "That's it. He took my phone."

Letting out a long sigh, Vice Principal Lopez turns to Shrey. "Mr. Malhotra?"

Shrey bounces from foot to foot. "I saw Ethan logged in as the Ella Baker Shade. He was writing a new post. When I read what he wrote, I grabbed the phone and ran here as fast as I could."

Principal El-Sayed's eyebrows shoot up toward her Halloween-themed hijab. "Ethan," she says. "Is this true?"

Ethan turns completely red, but stays silent, shooting dagger eyes at us.

"I'm going to need to check your phone, or call your parents if we can't sort this out. So you need to tell us the truth now," she says.

When he doesn't answer again, Principal El-Sayed delicately turns on the phone, which is thankfully still unlocked. It makes me wonder if Shrey messed with the settings, or if Ethan made the mistake of keeping it un-locked. That wouldn't fit Ella Baker Shade's profile.

After a heavy silence, she hands the phone over to Vice Principal Lopez. I see his eyes scan the screen for a few seconds before he looks up and says, "Mr. Navarez. I think we need to talk."

***

"Totally worth it!" Trissa exclaims as the three of us leave Vice Principal Lopez's office a half hour later. "One day in-class detention. They might not even bother calling Mama. Well . . . they probably will. But still!"

"I'm sure Dadi's Spidey sense is telling her that I got in trouble," Shrey says. "But catching Ethan was worth it. Did you see the look on his face when Principal El-Sayed turned on his phone?"

"Yeah, how was it still unlocked by the way?" I ask.

Shrey cracks his knuckles. "Just a brief journey into autolock settings. While I was running, by the way."

"Ha!" I shout. "I knew it."

Trissa giggles. "I can't believe we caught Ella Baker Shade!"

"I can't believe you two got the evidence to back it up!" I say. "How did you get his phone? I can't even tell you how perfect your timing wa—oof!" I exclaim, as we round the hallway corner, running straight into a grim-looking clown. "Pardon me, sir," I say in a silly voice. All three of us crack up, but the look on Ms. Marika's face chastens me as we enter the front office.

"Fall Fest just started," Ms. Marika tells Shrey and Trissa stiffly. "Since the school day is technically over, Principal El-Sayed let me know that you can wait with your friend until she's picked up. Your detentions are scheduled for next Monday, when we return from break, so you can feel free to attend Fall Fest. Drew, you may *not* come back on campus for the day."

Yikes. I guess it's possible she'll *never* trust me again after this. Which I deserve.

"Thanks, Ms. Marika," I say in a small voice as my friends exchange cringey looks. We both push through the double doors and collapse by the columns near the pickup area.

After spending one full minute enjoying the feeling of the sun on my face, I turn to Shrey and Trissa. "I can't believe you did it," I say again.

"I can't either," Shrey says. "But after I got your text, I found Trissa, and . . . it actually all came together."

"We were talking about your gazillion apology texts, and whether we should find you," Trissa continues. "Even though I still think what you did was *super* shady."

"It was!" I agree, my face reddening. "I really am sorry . . ."

Trissa gives Shrey an amused look. "Yeah. We kind of got that from your epic letter."

"Twelve pictures of handwritten sorries." Shrey adds. "*Twelve*. Have you heard of texting?"

I let out a small laugh, but still feel tears prickling at the corners of my eyes. "Okay. I'm also sorry about making you read my old-school loopy handwriting. But I wanted you to know."

Trissa gives me a playful shove, and this time it doesn't feel as weird. "You're okay, Nancy Drew. To be honest, I'm too excited about catching the Shade to be mad right now."

"YES," Shrey agrees. "Can we tell you about our heroic save now, by the way? Thank GOD Ethan didn't rat me out with the full story."

"Yes," I say. "Tell me, tell me."

"Okay," Trissa says. "So, there we are, standing on the blacktop and talking about what a *jerk* you are."

"I said bucket," Shrey interjects.

"Yeah, you did. Which I still don't get. But, anyway,

we also thought that maybe we should forgive you because your life is impossible right now. All that stuff about your dad. It didn't excuse the profiles, but it explained it."

"Thanks."

"Yeah. Anyway, Shrey and I are thinking: is Drew really going through with the whole heist thing? And, like you said, what are the chances that Ella Baker Shade doesn't post something new for Fall Fest?"

"That was technically a lie to throw the attention off the Dad stuff." I interject. "I thought if you found out about the PTO meeting, it would keep snowballing until you found out about the terrible thing I did. Which, you know, you *did*."

"I put that together, actually," Trissa says with a wink. "I might be an even better detective than you, Nancy Drew! But what you said about Fall Fest made sense. It's a big day."

"Trissa thought he might schedule the post for later," Shrey says. "But then I remembered something." He reaches into his pocket and grabs his phone and shows me the screen.

At first, I only see the loading screen for Amazon Kindle. But then I let out an audible gasp. "Wait, *what*? You downloaded *In the Shadow of a Killer*?"

Shrey rolls his eyes. "Uh, yeah. Of course I did. I bought it a month ago. It was obviously the only way I could speak 'Drew,' so—"

"You. Bought. Lita's. BOOK!"

"Yes, but that's not the heroic part. I remembered one part where Lita talks about organized offenders. She said something about how killers need to feel directly involved, even insert themselves into the crime scene. Then, I remembered your profile. You said that Ella Baker Shade might want to walk right into the chaos when the post went live. Which totally makes sense if Ethan is the type of person to sneak his name into a Shade post. I figured he'd want to be there when kids saw the post, whispering and laughing at the festival."

"That's when we got lucky," Trissa breaks in. "We saw Ethan on the far side of the blacktop, lurking by that one table. You know—the faded red one that all the birds use as a bathroom? Nobody sits there anymore. Anyway, he was staring at his phone. So, Shrey and I decided to follow him."

Shrey puffs out his chest proudly. "I followed him all the way into the bathroom. The bathroom, Leclair. Where the poop is. He was standing up against the side wall, past the urinals. But I got real close to slide around him and into a stall. When I passed, I saw him logged in to the Ella Baker Shade account! Before I knew it, I was knocking the phone out of his hand. He was surprised, so I grabbed it off the bathroom floor—risking a *zillion* poop germs, by the way. Then I used all of my base-running speed to get me to the office. And the rest is history!"

"They're gonna write folk songs about this one," Trissa says with a giggle.

"The heeero of Baaaaker, the man they call *Shreeeeeyyyyy!*" I sing. We all crack up, and for a moment, I actually feel like a regular kid laughing with her friends.

"All right," Trissa says, standing, "I'm supposed to catch up with my friend Liz by the candy corn tub. Is it okay if I bail?"

For the first time all day, I actually notice the familiar sights and smells of Fall Fest. The general sweetness in the air (likely due to the candy corn tub), elaborately carved pumpkins, hay bales, and festive games set up around campus almost make me regret doing this whole file room heist today. But not quite.

"Go meet Liz," I tell her, but quickly add, "Hey. Are you interested in coming over during break? What about

Halloween? Shrey and I usually hand out candy at my house. Maybe we could invite Connor and Holly, too. You know, to celebrate the downfall of the Shade? If we're okay, that is."

"We're okay," Trissa assures me. "But if you cross me again, *nope*." She tries to give me an intimidating look, but both of us end up giggling, since Trissa doesn't have an intimidating bone in her body.

"I promise," I tell her.

"Then I'll see you on Halloween," she says brightly. "Or Ahsoka Tano will see you on Halloween, that is."

Once Trissa disappears into the crowd, a long silence stretches between me and Shrey. Especially when I realize we're alone for the first time since I ditched him on the street last week.

"Um, Drew?" he says finally.

"Yeah?"

"Can I ask you something right now—and can it not turn into another huge fight? Because I don't think I could take another one."

"All right."

"It's about, you know . . . the kissing thing."

Suddenly, I hate Trissa. She clearly left on purpose, and I was too blinded by her shiny flip sequins and forgiving smile to see her devious plan. Closing my eyes, I sigh heavily. "All right," I repeat.

"I mean, I don't have to ask if you don't want me to. We can pretend none of this ever happened. It's . . . ugh."

"Shrey! Just ask already."

"Okay. So. Um, are you telling me the truth about not being ready for dating? Is it me?"

My insides do a pretzel twist, but I try to give him the best answer I can. "No. It's not you. I don't know what to tell you. I'm just not *there*."

Shrey's face falls. "Okay, but—and please don't take this the wrong way—you act so much older. You're obsessed with old-people television like *A Crime to Remember*, and you complain about potholes like a senior citizen. I guess I thought you might be lying because you think I'm hideous or something."

"Shrey. Come on, dude. You're empirically attractive. You're tall, symmetrical, you have sports muscles . . ."

"But you don't think I'm attractive."

"It's not that! I *think* you're attractive. But I have no desire to kiss you. I have no desire to kiss *anyone*."

"Okay. I mean . . . I thought for a while there, that . . . never mind."

"What?"

"That you might be into Trissa?"

That I was not expecting. "What? Why would you think that?"

Shrey sucks in another breath. "Because all of a sudden, she was there all the time. And it's not as if I don't like her. I do! I guess I thought that, even with your Han Solo thing . . . that this might be about boys in general."

"No, it's not just boys in general!" Feeling my voice get to a crabby place, I make an effort to settle it. "Look, if you're asking me to guess, I'll probably fall somewhere in the middle. You know, boys and girls. But I don't even know that. It's embarrassing, Shrey. Everywhere I go, people tell me that I'm an old soul. Then I look around, and I see people kissing and holding hands and stuff, and . . . I don't know. It grosses me out right now. Making out seems like people asking to wipe their snot on each other or something. Maybe I'm not the old soul everyone thinks I am."

He lets out a long and resigned sigh. "Okay."

"Can I ask *you* something?" I broach hesitantly.

He reddens but says, "Sure."

"Why do you like me? I mean, when did it change from like into the *Like* realm?"

Shrey reddens deeply, and at first I think he might

be incapable of speech. But then he stutters, "Umm, I—I like you because . . . because I *like* you, I guess. It just happened."

My throat feels dry as I swallow. "But you know me so well. You've known me all this time, through the moon-face era, and you have to sit less than two feet away from me when I get stressed and start, like, randomly farting. Shrey. You've seen me eat marzipan directly from a pastry tube. Is this really what you want?"

He looks sad. "Yeah."

"All right," I say, taking a deep breath. "But I have to be honest with you. I like our friendship the way it is. I think our friendship is better than kissing. Way better."

He takes a deep breath, looking suddenly winded, but nods.

"And, Shrey? Believe it or not, I do understand. Nobody knows better than me how it feels to . . . want a connection with someone and not have that returned."

Realization hits Shrey, and he looks immediately uncomfortable. "Yeah, I mean, of course you do."

"But you shouldn't have tried to kiss me without asking first."

Shrey turns pink from his cheeks all the way to the tips of his ears. "Wow. I didn't think about that. At *all*."

246

"I don't, like, blame you or anything. I think I'm just a person who, if I *am* ever interested in kissing, I'd want to be asked."

"Okay." Shrey hasn't quite returned to his usual color, but he sounds less nervous when he turns to me and says, "I'm really sorry, Drew. For all of it."

I'm about to reply, when I feel a sharp vibration at my hip. It's a text:

DAD: I will be there in FIVE minutes. I can't believe I left my phone in the prep room. DON'T MOVE.

"Well. That's going to suck," I say, showing him the text.

"Probably," he admits. "But maybe he'll give you a break. If there's any time to play the whole Mom-abandonment card, it's now."

"Maybe."

"Seriously, you can't be grounded. We still have to play *Legend of Zelda: Link's Awakening*, and our *Avatar* rewatch, and—hey!" Shrey breaks off, craning his neck over his right shoulder. He punches my arm. "Look!"

I spin around and peer toward the front office door, where Shrey is looking. Gasping, I realize that he's looking at a hunched and grim-looking Ethan Navarez.

OBSERVATIONS:

- Ethan looks even smaller than usual as he's escorted through the doors, and his eyes are streaked with tears.
- He clutches his binder, emblazoned with the same yearbook image that tipped me off.
- Our campus security guard is leading him, with a *super* serious look, toward an idling car in the parking lot.

CONCLUSION: Ethan Navarez is in deep, *deep* trouble.

"Yikes," Shrey says as we watch Ethan walk toward the dark green SUV. "Do you think he's going to get expelled?"

"Unlikely," I say with an air of false authority. "They never expel people here."

Shrey gulps. "So, we're going to have to *see* him after this? After the whole bathroom-phone thing?"

"Probably."

Ethan catches sight of us, and his inscrutable look is

the last thing we see before he disappears into the back seat of the car, which drives away with a squeal.

Shrey gulps. "That's not ideal."

"It is *not*," I agree. "But, hey, you caught the bad guy, right? What do you need to be afraid of?"

"Revenge?" Shrey offers. "I mean, aren't you worried? I got his phone, sure, but he knows it was you who figured him out."

"Maybe," I say with a sly smile. "I don't know. Lately I'm thinking that Ethan just made a bad decision. Maybe he'll actually learn from it. But if he does try anything, I've got my best friend to look out for me, right?"

Shrey grins back at me. "You always did."

25

TWENTY MINUTES LATER, Dad has cleaned his glasses approximately one billion times.

Well, okay, five. But still.

"So."

"So."

He was uncharacteristically silent when he drove me home from school, which set my nerves on end more than I care to admit. But then I saw three baguettes in the back seat. Dad doesn't get me baguettes when he's mad. He only gets baguettes when I'm sad—or for Murder and Mayhem nights. I obviously prefer the second one, but right now I'll take either.

"So."

Uncharacteristically, I'm the one who breaks our game of "so" chicken. "Dad? I'm really sorry."

He takes a deep breath, and for a moment, I'm sure he's about to clean his glasses for the two billionth time. Instead, he rips off the end of a seeded sourdough baguette and hands it over.

"Just . . . tell me what's going on."

I consider stuffing my mouth with bread until I'm physically unable to answer. But I know even carbs can't save me now. "Okay. You know how you said no one would know about Mom and Mr. Clark?"

"Yes."

Taking a deep meditative breath, I tell him—everything. From that first day with the kids laughing after Ella Baker Shade's post to deleting the message from Lopez, then all the way through my investigation. When I take out my phone to show him the two Instagram posts and the message, he flinches.

"I'm sorry," I tell him, my eyes welling up with tears. "I really didn't want you to see that."

Dad brings me in for a tight hug. "No, sweetie. It's not that. I can't believe you had to deal with this. This must have been impossible for you."

"But mostly because I was worried about you!" I insist. "I thought if I didn't catch Ethan before you went to the PTO meeting tonight, Mr. Lopez would tell you everything and you'd be back to being sad again. And when you talked about how focused I was on my new friends, I felt like I'd abandoned you when you needed me the most."

"Oh, sweetheart," Dad says with a sad expression, "I'm probably going to cry now, but please don't take it the wrong way. Believe me when I say that my emotional outburst that night had nothing to do with you."

"Really?"

"Nope. I was crying because I'm sad, Drew. Because I miss your mom. Even though I don't want to. The thing is, I lost a partner. It was just regular old . . . what's that word you use for bad-normal?"

"Beige?"

"Yeah. Beige sadness. It had nothing to do with you tracking down some cyberbully."

"Oh."

"And it certainly had nothing to do with you making new friends," Dad adds. "To be honest, when I came home to find you having fun . . . well, that was the happiest I've been since she left."

I swat at an errant tear. "Me too."

"I'm so glad."

"But you're still my *best* friend. Officially."

"Same, honey. But I've got to be your dad, too. Which

is why I decided not to join the PTO. Or to try and do everything your mom did. I have more important things to focus on."

"Yeah," I say. "You've got Leclair's . . ."

"Drew. By important things, I mean *you*."

"Me?"

Dad gives me a disbelieving look. "Yeah. You, dork!"

I smile and give him a little shove.

Dad tousles my hair affectionately. "I need to make sure you're surrounded by support. I'm sure that Grandma Joy and your cousins down in Culver City will still be in touch. But it might be awkward with your only extended family related to Mom."

Instinctively, I rush to tell him: "Oh, I'll be fine! Don't worry about me, I swear!"

Dad sets his jaw and levels me with a knowing look. "Drew. You were bullied badly enough that you started profiling your classmates. Your mother is not around right now, and you're having problems with your best friend. And the events of the last few weeks as a whole—"

"Stank?" I offer. "Stank like nine-day-old cheese Danish?"

"Well, let's say this: life is lumpy," Dad tells me

thoughtfully. "Life doesn't care whether you've had a bad week, or year. It brings what it brings. But good things can happen the same way."

The words spill out of my mouth before I can stop them: "So, Mom's never coming back. Is she?"

Dad lifts his mouth in an apologetic smile. "I know this is hard, Drew. I can't tell you when or if your mom will come back."

"Okay."

"But I do know she loves you very much."

"*Sure* she does."

"She does, Drew. I know you must not feel it. And it might be easier to think of your mom as a villain in all of this. But she hasn't had the easiest time of it. We never talk about your Grandpa Roy because he passed when you were little, but he wasn't the nicest or warmest man. He didn't show her a lot of love, or let her be a real kid. She never really dealt with that, and then you were born."

"Um, not *my* fault!" I protest.

"Trust me, I'm not saying it is. I'm just saying your mom didn't get much of a childhood. In some ways, neither have you because of your illnesses. But you make it your business to act older and more mature. *You* try to figure people out and what makes them tick. I don't think your mom ever got over not having a stable childhood. I think it makes her want to run away and be childish sometimes. But, sweetheart, I promise: she loves you with all her heart. We *both* do."

"It doesn't excuse what she did."

Dad lets out a measured breath. "Of course it doesn't. When I think about what she did to me, I'm mad enough. But, knowing what this did to *you* these past few weeks? I can't even talk about how furious I am right now."

"Why don't you say it? How mad you are, I mean."

"Because I'm your dad. And, no matter how badly she messed up, she *is* your mom."

I'm about to say something else—maybe snark so hard that I form a whole *puddle* of sarcasm by my feet. But what he's saying makes a tiny bit of sense, when I'm forced to think about it. Maybe I have been thinking of Mom as a villain. Hadn't I profiled her and even compared her to the Junipero Valley *Killer*? I never even thought about why she left, other than her selfishness. I guess I can't blame her for wishing she had the chance to be a real kid. But I can be mad at her for leaving. The thoughts swirl in my head, and it's not long before the tears come back.

"Ugh," I moan, wiping my face irritably. "Whatever. None of this would be happening if I'd been able to stick to my plan."

An arched eyebrow tells me Dad is intrigued. "Plan?"

"You know, my think-like-a-profiler plan."

"And this plan is . . . ?"

"I thought that if I could be Lita—like a scientist, you know—I could get us through this. I mean, you remember what she says about profilers, right? 'There has to be a healthy level of emotional detachment in order to do the job.' But now look at me! I'm a crybaby, too. I'm Daughter of Crybaby: The Revenge!"

"Oh, sweetie," Dad says, pulling me in for another hug. "You are dead wrong. I can't believe you've read that book three hundred times—I've only read it once, by the way—and you totally missed the point."

"What?"

"*In the Shadow of a Killer*," Dad says with a knowing smile. "We both know it's right there in your backpack. Give it to me—I'll show you what I mean."

Frowning, I unzip my bag and remove the now-tattered copy of *In the Shadow of a Killer*, giving it to Dad. He opens the book to the table of contents and then turns a few more pages until a self-satisfied grin spreads over his face. He hands me the book and points.

"All right," I say, skimming the words in front of me. It's the very same words I was just quoting, but . . . they're different than I remember.

Profiling and Emotion: Don't Get It Twisted

Most people will tell you that shutting off emotions is necessary to be an effective criminal profiler. When it comes to approaching victims and taking in crime scenes, this is certainly true. But, as for emotion altogether? I, for one, am tired of the "cold and detached" criminal psychologist trope.

Emotions can get us in trouble if we find ourselves overrelating to a case, but they also make us the best investigators we can be. Emotions and instincts go hand in hand, and a profiler needs instincts. Otherwise, I'm sure a number of very nice computers could do the job twice as well and three times as fast. I never would have chased the leads that tracked down the Junipero Valley Killer without a few healthy doses of fear, obsession, doubt, and—yes, even anger. It's human to feel emotions, and don't let anyone tell you differently.

I'm quiet for a long time before I speak again.
"Dad?"
"Yes, sweetie?"
"I don't think I want her to come back this time."
The confession brings another fresh round of tears,

and I let out full-fledged sobs until my throat burns and snot runs down the front of my face. They were the words I'd told myself so casually after she left, but now it feels real. Because I don't want someone living in our house who thinks we're weird and creepy. I don't want to live with someone who's always going to be wishing I'd turned out differently and who blames me for it. No matter what her reasons.

"I love you, sweetie," Dad says after my sobs eventually die down and I'm whimpering into his shoulder. "Times a *splabillion*. And I'm proud of you for trying to deal with Mom leaving in your own brilliant and completely unique way."

"Really?"

"Yeah. That being said, I *did* school you on *In the Shadow of a Killer.* Right?"

"You schooled no one!" I put on a mad face, but I'm relieved to get back to the part with more jokes and less unhinged sobbing. It's the part that makes sense to me.

"These past few days, is that what you've been trying to do? With the investigation and everything else? Trying to act like a profiler so you wouldn't feel bad about Mom leaving?"

"Maybe?" A rush of embarrassment flushes my

cheeks, but it's too late: I can already feel the babbling coming on: "I know—but I thought I would be better at it! It only didn't work because Shrey and I kept fighting, and then Mom called—"

"Mom called? Why didn't you tell me?"

I wave a hand dismissively. "Because I knew it would be a whole conversation. I kept trying to keep it down, but I guess I finally lost it today."

"You mean the call to your mother?"

Cringing, I nod. "They told you all that, huh?"

"Yep."

"Ugh! It's frustrating because I thought I was managing the whole 'conceal, don't feel' thing better than Elsa from *Frozen*, but then I totally flipped out! Like Elsa!"

Dad rips off another piece of baguette and hands it to me. "Oh, honey," he says, "I've got more bad news for you. You not only missed the entire point of *In the Shadow of a Killer*, you missed the point of *Frozen*."

My jaw drops. "Oh, man. You're right! The whole point of that movie is that Elsa thinks concealing her emotions will solve everything, but it makes everything worse. Almost-killing-her-*family* worse."

"Yep," Dad affirms. "And maybe—just maybe—you were trying too hard to avoid emotions and they built up. Like Elsa."

I don't know why, but the air in the room suddenly feels a thousand percent lighter. My body, which has been tense all day, is starting to relax.

Well, until Dad gives me a searching look that spells trouble.

"Heeeeyyyy."

"Hey?"

"So, I know I'm your dad, but I have to put that on pause for a second, okay?"

My eyes narrow into suspicious slits. "Okay."

Dad tents his hands and brings them to a point at his chin, as if he's barely containing some kind of juicy secret. "Because you are in trouble at school, and I don't want you to think I'm condoning *anything* you've done. But I've been dying to ask. When I called Vice Principal Lopez back, he didn't only tell me about your file heist and the very loud message you left for your mom. He told me something else—something *amazing*."

"Dad! Spit it out!"

"He said you made a crime board. Is it true?"

I lower my head. "Yes."

"Okay, okay. So, this is where punishing you gets difficult, because I'm too proud. Did you really show the principal of Ella Baker Middle School a detailed *profile* of this cyberbully? And what does the crime board look like? Is there color coding? Wait, don't tell me. I know you—there's color coding."

"Ugh," I moan. "Do you want to see my crime board?"

"Do I want to see your crime board? Do I *want* to see your *crime* board . . ."

"Fine! I'll get it!"

Dropping the chunk of baguette I haven't quite finished, I plod down the hall into my room, at which point I feel a vibration from my phone. It's Dad, of course. He's sending me a text that says *Crime board* = with several enthused GIFs that *almost* make me laugh.

"You're the WORST!" I shout down the hall.

"I love you too-ooo!" he shouts back in a singsong voice.

When I drag the crime board out from under my bed and present it to him, he practically has stars in his eyes.

"Wow," he marvels, scanning my work. "I always figured you would grow out of the whole true crime thing one day. But this is really good, Drew. *Really* good."

"I guess I am okay . . ." I trail off and give him a sly look. "Maybe you can remarry with Lita Miyamoto someday and we can be a crime-solving family!"

Dad guffaws, finally prying his gaze away from the crime board. "Uh, no. That woman is way out of my league."

I stomp my foot playfully. "But she loves chocolate! And you *make* chocolate. I don't see how I can make this any simpler for you."

"Approximately twenty billion women love chocolate, Drew."

"Fine. As long as you pick someone who doesn't hate my creepy interests or insist you get me into kid activities like *soccer*." I spit out the word as if it tastes bad. "Look, I *could* be okay with you marrying Karrie or Grace from *Crime and Waffles*. That could work too. I'm not picky."

"Yeah . . . you're definitely *not* picky." He levels his gaze at me dubiously and then both of us bust up laughing again.

"So," I say when our laughter dies down. "What now?"

Dad smiles, taking off his glasses and cleaning them. Somehow, it doesn't seem as ominous this time. "Well," he says. "Now that the whole crime board thing is out of my system, I might need to work on treating you less like a friend and more like my kid for a while."

I frown. "I don't know how I feel about that."

"It doesn't mean we can't watch *Trail of Blood*. Only that you're my daughter first. It has to be that way; otherwise I'm going to totally mess you up."

I bite my lip thoughtfully. "All right. Let's aim for only *slightly* messing me up."

Dad laughs at my corny joke, even though it kind of sucks. "Tonight, we should probably wallow, though. And consume a metric ton of chocolate and true crime."

The idea makes me feel warm, like the insides of a freshly baked chocolate croissant. I smile at him and say, "Perfect."

26

"WELL, ETHAN NAVAREZ is officially suspended," Trissa announces two days later, on Halloween night. I'd barely let Trissa in the door and led her to our living room when she bursts out with the news.

"Wait, what?" I ask, whiplashed. "How do you know that?"

Trissa tents her hands conspiratorially, which looks even more ominous with her striped orange Ahsoka Tano makeup. "Well. I found out from Liz, who knows Ethan's sort-of friend Shawn."

"What's a sort-of friend?" I ask.

"I dunno. They game together or something. Ethan apparently told Shawn his whole plan right before Fall Fest. He said that he had a foolproof plan to pin the posts on Johnny Granday to get him in trouble. I guess the plan was sending you that message? Anyway, Shawn said that he tried to call Ethan, but his parents said he's on virtual lockdown for being suspended. As in: he can't use computers *or* phones!" Trissa breaks out in a cackle. "Isn't that just *perfect*?"

I bite my lip. The truth is, part of me does feel for Ethan after everything that happened. Nobody knows what it's like to obsess over bullies and justice more than I do. That being said, he took that obsession to a dark place and hurt people. And the thought of Ethan having to sit at home weaving a basket (or something equally screen-free) does make me smile—just a little.

"Oh!" Trissa adds. "And there's something else! At the end of Fall Fest the other day, I saw Vice Principal Lopez walk up to Johnny Granday while he was with his friends. And he looked *dead* serious."

I feel my eyes widen. Is it possible that Trissa, Shrey, and I did exactly what we set out to do? Could our school life actually *change* after this?

Brrrriiiinnngggg!

"That must be Shrey and Connor," I explain to Trissa as I walk toward the front door. "Shrey said he was planning to walk up the hill with him since they're neighbors. I'm not sure if Holly is coming or not. Her mom made it sound like she was trying to convince her."

Trissa casts a furtive glance toward the kitchen.

Laughing, I say, "Go get your cereal. I know you want to."

She doesn't need to be told twice.

When I walk toward the doorway, I have a brief flash of Mom standing there, a week and a half ago—with her packed bags and her sad face. But this time it doesn't hurt so much. My house isn't a crime scene anymore. It's my home, with my dad. It's the place where I can welcome my friends.

Friends! *Plural!*

When I finally open the door, I can't help but gasp in surprise. Holly is standing in my doorway. In contrast to pretty much every day at school, where she hides behind her hair, Holly is wearing a fitted black dress. Her hair is piled high on her head in a glamorous updo, and she wears a sparkling tiara and black heels.

"Whoa, Holly! You look amazing!" I exclaim.

Blushing, she says, "Thanks. I love Audrey Hepburn. My mom and I stayed up all night making it. You like?"

"I love!" It's amazing how much happier and more confident Holly looks outside of school. We texted a lot over the last few days—enough that she'd admitted to commenting on Micah's post, but deleting it when she realized how mean it sounded. Holly was never Ella

Baker Shade material, and I can't believe I thought for a second that it could be her.

I wave a hand to usher Holly inside, craning my neck as I spot Shrey and Connor heading up the walkway. "Come on in!" I call.

Connor is dressed up as Captain America, so I give him a patriotic salute as he passes me by. As soon as I take in Shrey's costume, my jaw drops in horror. "What is *that*?"

Shrey, who wears a green and yellow Rickey Henderson jersey from the Oakland A's, looks down at his "costume" and back up at me. "What?"

I wrinkle my nose. "A sports outfit?"

"You're wearing leggings!" He protests. "And they're called costumes, not outfits."

"Are you two fighting again?" Dad breaks in. He peeks his head through the door and makes a noise. "A baseball costume? *Someone's* phoning it in."

I wave a hand toward my dad. "See?"

"Whatever," Shrey says, rolling his eyes. "Is Trissa here yet?"

"She's in the kitchen, cereal hunting obviously."

"Oooh, Cake Flakes!" Shrey says with bright eyes. He moves past me and heads for the kitchen. I'm about to follow him when Dad stops me.

"Where's your costume?" he asks.

I smack my head. "Oh, yeah. I keep forgetting. Can you be the host for a few minutes while I get dressed?"

He tousles my hair. "Will do. I'm really glad to see you having fun with your friends, and I can't wait to get to know Holly and Connor. But don't forget to pack tonight, okay?"

"I won't."

After Tuesday, Dad decided that we needed a *real* break. So, he's taking us on a last-minute trip to Southern California. He worked it out with Mr. Lopez and everything—I won't be starting my in-school suspension until next Thursday. After his whole I-have-to-be-your-dad-first realization, he reached out to Grandma Joy. It will be nice to see her and all my little cousins and Aunt Lucy. But I *really* hope they don't defend Mom.

"By the way," Dad says, a sly expression creeping over his face. "Before I give your friends the tour, I've got a surprise."

"What?"

He leads me down the hallway toward my room with a hand on my back.

"Un*hand* me, old man!" I yell. "What surprise?"

When we get to my room, he gestures to my laptop

and says, "You know how your grandma lives by Griffith Park?"

"Yeahhhh."

"Well, there's also a Twilight Books near there. And . . ."

"What?"

Dad's self-satisfied smile is actually killing me right now. He sits down on my bed, grabs my copy of *In the Shadow of a Killer,* and flips through it almost casually.

"DAD. Are you the Junipero Valley Killer right now? Because you are actually *killing* me."

Dad laughs and then holds up his phone. On the screen, a Reddit alert appears. The post reads

/r/IntheShadowofaKiller
CALIFORNIA ALERT! For those of you willing to make the trek, our own Lita Miyamoto is doing a reading from IN THE SHADOW OF A KILLER at Twilight Books in Los Feliz, announced yesterday! This impromptu signing and reading will be on Saturday at 7 p.m. Hope to see all you Lita stans there!

"WHAT?" I cry. I immediately start bouncing on the bed excitedly. Once I stop long enough to remain steady,

I envelop Dad in a big hug. "How did I not know about this?"

"Well, that's what you get for ignoring your true crime feed," Dad clucks.

"So . . . we're really going? And then you'll marry Lita, and we can become a crime-solving family?"

"Not that last part, but yes. We're really going."

I hug Dad even tighter, until what he says next. "There is one thing I need you to do first. You're going to have to call your mom."

"What? Like, before we go to LA?"

His eyes are uncharacteristically serious as he says, "Yes, before LA. We can't have this hanging over us. Especially not after the message you left on Tuesday. She's tried to call you three times already."

Okay. Maybe I do need to call her. But what am I supposed to say?

Hey, Mom. I hope you and Dustin fall into a volcano. Hugs and kisses!

Hey, Mom. I'm mega-beige now, so come home!

Hey, Mom. A restraining order is in process. Please refrain from any contact, or you will hear from my lawyer. PS: I HATE YURTS!!!

Sigh.

"Okay," I finally whisper in reply. "But let me get it over with now. I don't want to be thinking about it all night."

"Good plan."

"Can I be alone?"

He rests a hand on mine. "Yeah, Bun. I'll get your friends started on a movie. Take all the time you need."

For a long moment, I simply stare at my phone. Feeling unable to make the call, I decide to procrastinate by getting into my costume. I decided to go as Nancy Drew, as a little nod to Trissa and Dad. Unfortunately, it doesn't take me long to pull on the plaid skirt and put on the orange bobbed wig necessary for the costume. I pick up the signature magnifying glass to top it off and tap the edge on my desk nervously while my phone taunts me, its screen gleaming ominously a foot away.

I'm ready to completely disobey Dad and forget it, but a surge of courage pushes me to snatch the phone and dial Mom's number. I'm super relieved when I get her voicemail, but then I realize I have to leave another message. What am I supposed to say after the last time?

"Ummmm, hi, Mom," I stumble after I hear the beep. "It's Drew. I mean . . . I guess you know who it is.

You haven't been gone long enough to forget my voice at least."

I squeeze my eyes shut. Less than ten seconds in, and I'm already blowing it.

"Look, I'm sorry for the message I left you the other day. I was really mad, but you probably know that. I'm *really* mad at you, Mom. I'm sorry I said all those things —about the files, though. It was really awful of me to read Mr. Cla—ehm, Dustin's notes. I hope you're sorry too. I mean, about leaving . . ." I take a deep breath and stare at *In the Shadow of a Killer* for strength as I add, "I love you, Mom. Bye."

As soon as I press the red button to end the call, I feel tears spilling down my cheeks. I use the pale blue cardigan from my Nancy Drew outfit to pat them dry and then stand.

Lita says that some cases never feel closed. I guess she felt that way a lot after catching the Junipero Valley Killer—like part of her wanted to keep searching. Maybe that's how it is with Mom. A case that will never feel closed. But calling her is a start.

"Drew," Dad's voice calls softly. "I don't want to interrupt, but Trissa asked me to tell you to, quote 'get your butt in the living room to watch horror movies' with them. I think she means business. Also, Connor

272

and Holly started singing songs from *Hamilton*. I just put on the soundtrack for them. I hope that's okay."

"Give me a minute!" I call back. I look around my room again, until I'm fully calm. Then I move for the door. When I do, something catches my eye: the stack of notebooks by my bed. The remaining four in a pack of five, they're still half encased in ripped plastic. As of Tuesday, when I wrote the apology letter for Shrey and Trissa, the last notebook was filled.

Casting a look back at my suitcase, I wonder: should I pack a new one? It seems like my notebooks mostly get me in trouble. And it's not like I'm going to spend my vacation spying on Grandma Joy. But the idea of being without it makes me feel like I'd be missing a part of me. Before I can talk myself out of it, I crack open the new book, feeling a jolt of delight as the spine stretches:

OBSERVATIONS:

- I want to hang out with my friends more than I want to watch *Trail of Blood*.
- They seem to actually want to spend time with me.

"Drew!" Shrey shouts from down the hall, his voice nearly drowned out by Holly and Connor's rendition of

"The Room Where It Happens." "What about 'get your butt in here' did you not understand?"

Smiling, I add.

CONCLUSION: Being creepy isn't so bad after all.

After I close the notebook, I tuck it into my suitcase. Maybe catching Ethan won't stop the bullies at Ella Baker Middle School completely. And maybe I'll never *really* be able to predict Mom's serial offenses. But the mystery of being two months into school with only one friend?

It's possible, like Lita said, that I changed the puzzle after all.

THE END

ACKNOWLEDGMENTS

First and foremost, I would like to thank my family. Ben and Mia, you are my entire heart. For this book, you both gave me the love and space I needed to write. Most of all, however, you've given me a truly beautiful life with you. To Dad (a.k.a. the real Sam Leclair), Mom (nothing like Jenn Leclair), and Maren: you always told me I was good enough, even from my first mystery books written as a child. Without each of you, my life would have been infinitely less fun—I love you all so very much! Many hugs as well to my found family. Thanks to Katie for fangirling out about each book, and at each step of this process. And, Karim, I owe you a debt of gratitude I can't even begin to list here. You've read and edited *every* one of my books, including these acknowledgments. Grazie mille!

Also, thanks from the bottom of my heart to my friends—my own Shreys and Trissas. I couldn't have done this without all of you. I want to give a special shout-out to my oldest friend, Adrienne, who got me through elementary school. The bullying aspect of this book is a very real part of my history. I don't think I could have made it through that, or write about it today, had you not been such a wonderful ally.

This book would not be what it is without my agent, the exceptional Chelsea Eberly. Your vision, editorial nature, and hard work pushed me to make this the absolute best version of my work it could be. I'm so lucky to have you in my corner. Thanks so much to Greenhouse Literary Agency, and to The Rights People for helping bring my work to readers around the world! I also would like to add that this book is a #DVpit success story. Thanks so much to Beth Phelan and everyone who works so tirelessly to provide this opportunity to historically marginalized creators.

I'm also endlessly grateful to my editor, Emilia Rhodes, whose enthusiasm (and similar true crime love) made me know right away she was the *perfect* fit for this book. I am indebted to many at Clarion Books who put their tireless effort into this book. A sincere thanks to

Elizabeth Agyemang, Mary Magrisso, and Catherine San Juan. I also want to express my appreciation for Naakai Addy and Tanu Srivastava. Your incredibly thoughtful insights helped bring this story to the next level.

Without beta readers and critique groups, I would have been writing in a vacuum. Never a good idea! Firstly, I am so thankful for my amazing critique partner, Eva. You are my writing soulmate, and I'm so glad we found each other. Thanks to Sa'iyda for reading a *very* early draft and telling me I was onto something. I'm so pleased that a beta request brought us together as friends! Also, a hat tip to my middle-grade critique group—Ellen, Alex, and Terrie—who helped me shape the opening pages right before I landed my agent. Lastly, a huge credit to Gregg Hurwitz. You took the time to sit on the phone with your old English teacher's daughter, and you told me to keep at it because I had what it takes. Your advice and mentorship have been invaluable these past years, and I deeply appreciate it.

There are two groups that were integral to my writing this book. First, thank you to librarians everywhere for being champions of those who tell their stories—especially those from a unique and often underrepresented point of view. Secondly, thanks to the murderino community. Without you, I would have never had the confidence to admit that I've been a true crime enthusiast since I was twelve, let alone write a book all about it!

Finally, thanks to my friend Jamin. I wrote my first book for you, and you'll always be in my heart.

DON'T MISS
THE NEXT DREW LECLAIR MYSTERY!

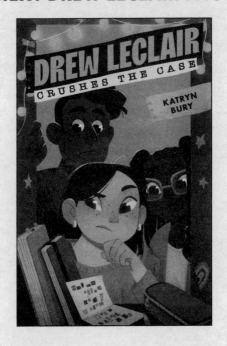

1

TWENTY-TWO GRAPES. That's how many it took for our school librarian, Mr. Covacha, to notice that something was afoot.

My best friend, Shrey, always rolls his eyes when I use words like *afoot*. "Drew," he says, "why are you always talking like those old British detectives?"

Okay, so he's not wrong.

But I knew something was up by the third grape. Three is kind of a magical number in criminal profiling. My hero, Dr. Lita Miyamoto, says that after three crimes you know a perpetrator doesn't just have a motive, they have an *obsession*.

Ever since the book fair preview last week, Mr. Covacha had been finding grapes around the fair. The weird thing? They were *single* grapes. One on the shelves, one by the register, and one balanced atop the pyramid-style book displays. When I volunteered to help around the fair, I started to find them too. Each grape was so far spread out that it was clear these kids weren't randomly dropping snacks.

This was *deliberate*.

It was all I could do not to track down the perpetrators myself. I kept reminding myself that I was under strict orders: no more snooping. Even when I'm *not* trying, though, the answers often find me.

First, I noticed that the grapes appeared only after sixth grade lunch. Yesterday, I'd casually noted to Mr. Covacha that I'd seen Dante King and Sukhjot Kaur at the book fair every day. But the final clue was too much for me to disregard. Today, I saw Dante and Sukhjot passing each other grapes when *mandarin oranges* were on the school lunch menu. I mean, you can't ignore that, right?

Still, it was hard to hand over the names to Mr. Covacha without explaining to him about the modus operandi. Not to mention the fact that the perpetrators were so clearly escalating. But school mysteries are something I promised to leave behind. Especially since, so far, they've only gotten me:

1) An in-school suspension

2) Ostracized by my peers

3) Forced to talk about my feelings every night with my dad, who I'd way rather be watching true crime documentaries with.

So, I'm doing the regular-kid thing. Which is why I'm watching Mr. Covacha perform the laziest interrogation I've ever seen in my years of watching detective shows.

"Hey, kiddos," he says, leaning over a nervous-looking Dante and Sukhjot. They're caught and they know it. "I know this is going to sound . . . well, a little silly. But, have you two been leaving grapes around the book fair this week?"

Squeezing my eyes shut, I imagined how it would be if I were asking the questions. In my mind, I would be like a British detective, declaring my deductive process as the suspects squirmed.

"A. Single. Grape," I would say emphatically, slowly pacing the displays. "In point of fact, *twenty-two* single grapes. To be fair, grapes *were* on the lunch menu that first day. But why, then, would the grapes be so deliberately placed? One grape on the graphic novels. One on the historical fiction display. One balanced between two *Fortnite* books." Then I would swing around, eyes wide, pointing at Dante. "*You* like *Fortnite*, don't you, Dante?"

A smile instinctively tugs at the corners of my mouth as I imagine myself with a Sherlock Holmes–esque cap, talking the perpetrators into a corner. But then, a real confession jerks me out of the fantasy.

"Okay!" Sukhjot says, looking up at Mr. Covacha with a frown. "We thought it would be funny!"

"We didn't think anyone would notice!" Dante jumps in. "It's not like we took anything, or ruined any books. I mean, kids are stealing erasers all the time! And I know one kid took the big World Records book! I'm pretty sure I saw him do it."

My ears perk up at this. I'd noticed that book missing a few days ago, and I knew that Mr. Covacha already suspected someone. I swear, I don't *mean* to overhear conversations. Sometimes it just happens.

From behind the counter, I stare at Mr. Covacha, willing him to ask a follow-up question.

"I see," Mr. Covacha says, rubbing his chin as if he's trying to figure out what to ask next. "Well . . ."

I feel as if my head might explode.

Ask him who did it! He knows! Just ASK!

Fortunately, Dante is more than willing to blab without Mr. Covacha's help.

"It was a big kid," Dante tells him. "He's white, with blond hair and a really pink face. Like he's embarrassed or blushing or something—but all the time."

I mentally keep track of the details. *White, pinkish complexion, tall or heavyset* . . . That totally fits with Aiden Rullhausen—the kid I'd overheard Mr. Covacha talking about with Vice Principal Lopez.

"Okay, Alan. Thanks for telling me that," Mr. Covacha says.

"We're sorry, Mr. Covacha," Sukhjot and Dante say in unison.

Then, after this complete nothing-burger of an interrogation, Mr. Covacha says, "Thanks, kiddos. You can go back to class. Just cut it out with the grapes, okay?" He walks behind the desk next to me and dismisses the two sixth graders with a wave.

When they've shuffled out, I turn to Mr. Covacha. I'm sure that my usually pale and freckled complexion is crimson due to the whole head-nearly-exploding from a few minutes earlier. So, I try to sound as casual as possible when I say, "Well, I guess it was that Aiden Rullhausen kid you thought it was. Who stole the Guinness World Records book, I mean."

Mr. Covacha gives me an appraising look over the tip of his glasses. "How did you know I thought it was Aiden?"

My face heats up, and I imagine I must be full tomato

color by now. "You talk pretty loud."

"You're very observant, aren't you, Drew?"

"Some say that," I tell him with a shrug. "Usually while they're yelling at me."

He laughs. "I like observant. It makes for a good librarian, you know. Think about it."

I've got another career path in mind, but I still beam up at him. "Thanks, Mr. Covacha."

He looks at his office. "All right, I'll give Vice Principal Lopez a call about that stolen book now. Will you be okay running the counter?"

I give him a thumbs-up and watch as he slips into his office and closes the door. I'd agreed to stay to help during lunch today, but the rush usually doesn't start for another ten minutes, until after kids eat their food. I reach into my backpack and pull out my notebook, opening it to a page I'd marked: *Book Fair Grape Prank*.

Even though I'm not *technically* solving mysteries right now, I like to keep good records. That can't get me in trouble, right?